THE
LAST
ONE

THE
LAST
ONE

CHERYL THOMAS

XULON ELITE

Xulon Press Elite
2301 Lucien Way #415
Maitland, FL 32751
407.339.4217
www.xulonpress.com

Paperback ISBN-13: 978-1-66286-241-0
Ebook ISBN-13: 978-1-66286-242-7

CHAPTER 1

Two young boys stood at one end of a very large, very elaborately decorated living room peering into a small crib where a tiny infant lay sleeping peacefully, a thumb near slightly parted lips ready to soothe him back to sleep at a moment's notice. It was hardly necessary, though, since this infant was already used to the noise and activity that was even now beginning to accelerate around him. He would not be bothered by anything less than hunger pangs or a soiled diaper. Since he had just been fed and changed, that was unlikely to happen for several hours.

The boys pondering this new arrival appeared to be twins about four or five years old. Although their faces were nearly identical, their expressions were not. The first was standing tiptoed on top of a pile of pillows, resting his chin on folded hands propped up by the crib railing. The curly blond hair and sweet smile reaching just past the top rail gave him a kind of angelic glow. He was humming softly and appeared enamored with the small, sleeping baby. The other twin had slightly darker, dirty-blond hair and a scowl to match. His hands were on his hips, his head slightly forward and pressed against the rails, as if he were about to scold the baby for coming into the world, for sleeping, or for just being. His eyes flashed with loathing as he glanced back and forth between the baby and the smiling boy. He opened his mouth to say just exactly what was on his mind.

"Sshh!" whispered Michael, the first twin. "We're supposed to be watching him, not waking him up."

Johnny, the second twin, scowled even more deeply. "I don't want to wake him up. I just want to kill him." He slowly extended a dirty arm between the rails of the crib.

"You can't," whispered Michael. "You're not even allowed to touch him."

"So what," Johnny retorted, curling his long bony fingers into a fist much too close to the baby's neck. "Neither are you." Just a few more inches, a few more moments, and it would be done.

"I don't need to touch him. I'm happy just watching him sleep." Michael sighed. "He's so tiny and so cute. Don't you think so?"

"No!"

Johnny's adamant opinion was barely out of his mouth when a shadow fell across the crib and two very plump hands with long, brightly colored finger nails at the end of wrinkled and freckled fingers reached out and pulled the twins away from the crib. Johnny's disgusted gaze traveled from those hideous hands to what he thought was an equally hideous face glaring back at him. The fat, middle-aged woman who had grabbed the twins bent over as far as she could and brought the boys up close to her face, her eyes narrowed and scowling.

"Whose boys are you?" she scolded. "You are going to wake little Christopher up with all that noise. Now scat! Go find your mother before you ruin the christening party. Tsk, tsk!"

She gave each a pat on their bottoms and one more shove before calling out exuberantly, "Yoo-hoo! Margarite! Over here! I'm so glad you were feeling well enough to come!" She waved enthusiastically at an even larger, older woman across the room before waddling away.

The twins moved back to their original positions, standing very still like tiny Buckingham Palace guards on opposite sides of the crib as people of all sizes and shapes and ages filled the room, chattering and laughing and making much more noise than the two boys had with their whispered conversation. Still, the baby lay peacefully, occasionally smiling in his sleep as people came and went, oohed and aahed, touched his tiny hands, kissed his forehead or crossed themselves saying, "He is the spitting image of his grandfather, God bless him."

The tired mother and proud father stood near Father Giovanni as aunts, uncles, cousins, and distant relatives twice removed filed by to kiss them, shake their hands, and give hearty hugs and unsought advice. They placed congratulatory cards containing large amounts of cash on a nearby table that was carefully monitored by Nonno, the baby's grandfather. This was a miracle child and everyone knew it. Nonno told the story every day to everyone he met and was never interrupted or hurried, even if his listeners had heard the story many times before.

"Congratulations Nonno!"

"He's the spittin' image of you, Nonno!"

"I never seen such a handsome boy, Nonno."

"You must be so proud, Nonno."

Everyone in the family stopped by the table to make sure Nonno knew they had come to this most important event. And everyone in the family smiled for Nonno, shook his hand, or gave him a kiss on both cheeks before they moved aside, poured themselves a glass of wine, ate a cannoli, and wondered how much longer they would have to grovel before Nonno. But, money was money and power was power and he had both. For now.

The wine was the best money could buy and was flowing freely among the guests. Of course, there were plenty of other drinks for those who preferred hard liquor. No expense had been spared to welcome this child into the world and christen his soul for God and for the church.

"Thank you for your gift."

"Very kind of you to come."

Nonno's responses to the guests were short but calculated. "Thank you for your gift" meant "You will be very sorry if you were not generous to my grandson" and "Very kind of you to come" meant "Very lucky for you that you showed up." Nonno had very little patience for most of the relatives. He knew what they were saying behind his back and couldn't care less. But for Teresa, his daughter-in-law, and for his son, Joseph, his feelings were genuine affection. For his wife, well, his feelings were mostly of fear, even though he had never let on in the 30 years they had been together. She seemed to have—or was very good at pretending to have—a connection to the supernatural that was quite eerie. But she was a good wife, a good cook, and a good listener whenever she took a break from talking.

His daughter-in-law, Mrs. Teresa D'Antoni, had bad ovaries, unable to make healthy eggs, doctors said. Useless. That had been Nonno's one complaint about his daughter-in-law. She could not provide an heir to his power and fortune. The D'Antoni name would die out, unless, of course, she died first and Joseph remarried a young, fertile woman. But then, after they had given up all hope—a miracle! As the last of the relatives arrived, Nonno stood and began The Story. The gossip, the flirting, the joking, and the complaining among the guests paused as Nonno's strong voice commanded their attention. Nonno was a natural storyteller and they listened, not just out of respect and fear, but because it was the story of a miracle.

Teresa believed it was the flu, at first. But when the flu lasted for three weeks, then four, she began to worry. The smell of beef made her throw up every time. She could no longer cook. Cleaning exhausted her. Before long, her husband Joseph was worried too. What good is an Italian wife who can't cook or clean? Who would take care of him? What to do? He called his Momma.

Momma made Nonno drive her to Joseph's house immediately so she could take care of her poor darling boy. Although they only lived about 15 minutes away from each other, she would move in with them for a while. That is, for as long as it took to fix everything. Momma tucked a picture of her friend's daughter, Maria, in her purse, just in case.

When Momma arrived, she took one look at her ghostly pale daughter-in-law, dropped her suitcases, threw her hands in the air and began wailing. Joseph and Nonno tried to calm her down. Teresa burst into tears and ran up the front steps, through the house, and into the first floor bathroom, slamming the door behind her and lunging for the toilet. She began vomiting loudly and violently. The men ignored Teresa and instead took Momma by the arms and gingerly led her into the house. She was sobbing hysterically, but allowed them to help her with her coat in the foyer and to dab her eyes with their initialed handkerchiefs. They guided her into the living room—the very living room where all the guests were now standing, listening to the story.

The guests nodded and looked around as if on holy ground as Nonno paused his narration. Satisfied with their reaction, he continued.

Momma grabbed Joseph's head and kissed every inch of his face, not satisfied until it was completely covered with red lipstick tracks.

"You poor, poor boy. Such a young man to be a widower! Why has God deserted me? I am a good, good woman with a good, good boy." Momma patted his cheeks. Her old Italian accent became thicker as she appeared to let grief overcome her. "Don' you worry, my son. Momma is here. I will take care of you." She made the sign of the cross in front of her ample bosom, checked her purse to make sure the picture of Maria was still there, then snapped it shut. "Now, where are the pots? I will make you lotsa pasta. You will feel better. Everything's a-gonna be alright. You see!" She hurried off to the kitchen and Joseph heard her opening and shutting cabinet doors, mumbling, "That girl, Teresa, she don't know how to organize a kitchen. I will fix it."

Joseph looked helplessly at his father. They both shrugged and settled in on two recliners situated comfortably in front of the TV.

"How are you doing, Pop?" Joseph asked.

"I'm OK," said Nonno. "You?"

"I'm OK too," said Joseph. "But Teresa… I'm worried. She's been sick a long time. She can't cook because the smells bother her. She throws up all day. She can't eat much, but she is still gaining weight. She cries all the time. I'm afraid she's gonna die but she won't even go to the doctor!"

Nonno looked thoughtful. "Hmmm. Your mother had those same symptoms once."

"Yeah?" Joseph looked hopeful. "And she got over it. She's fine now."

"Yeah. She got over it. In nine months she got over it."

"Nine months! What kind of flu takes nine months to get over?"

Nonno leaned over and smacked Joseph on the side of the head. "Did I really raise such an idiot? Nine months. Nine months. What takes nine months?"

Joseph looked puzzled.

Nonno sighed. "Your mother was pregnant with you when she had those symptoms. Teresa is pregnant."

"No, Pop. She can't have kids. You know that."

"OK. I'm an old man. I don't know nothing."

The bathroom door creaked. Teresa came furtively into the living room where her husband and father-in-law were talking. She looked awful. Her face was pale and swollen, her eyes were red from crying, and her hands were folded over her stomach in a futile attempt to hold back the next wave of nausea.

"I'm sorry, Pop. I'm just so emotional lately. I don't know what's wrong with me!" She wiped a tear with her sleeve.

Nonno reached out his arms and drew her close in a big bear hug. "That's OK, sweetheart. You're just gonna have a baby, that's all that's wrong with you."

Teresa pushed away from him. "That's mean, Pop. You know I can't."

"OK. Whatever you say. No baby for you."

"Baby? Who said baby?" Momma came into the room with a tray of steaming hot tea and cookies. She put the tray on the coffee table and stood with her hands on her wide hips. When no one would meet her eyes or answer her, she crossed her arms. "No one's gonna get any food unless they tell me what's going on here."

"Pop thinks Teresa's pregnant, Momma," said Joseph.

Momma turned to Teresa. She looked her up and down from across the room before moving with purpose over to where Teresa stood trembling with nausea, one hand over her mouth, the other over her stomach. As the men watched warily, Momma put her hands on Teresa's abdomen and raised her face to the ceiling, her mumbled incantations breaking the silence. Momma reached up and attempted to knead Teresa's swollen breasts. Teresa was frozen in surprise and, although she was unable to move, she was not unable to speak. "Ow! What are you doing? Stop! That hurts!"

Momma took Teresa's face between her hands and stared into her eyes. "Oh my god. Six years. Six years. Oh my god."

Teresa tried to talk but her lips were squeezed together between Momma's hands. She held onto Momma's wrists and tried to make her let go.

"Oh my god. Oh my god." Momma finally let go and sank to the couch, clutching her heart. Joseph jumped up from the chair. He sat beside her on the couch and took her hands. "Momma! Momma! What is wrong? Are you all right?"

Teresa, gagging, ran back into the bathroom and slammed the door. Momma put her head into her hands and began crying. "It's a miracle. It's a miracle!"

"That's what I said," said Nonno, smiling.

Nonno stood with his hands in the air, his story finished. There was a hushed silence before the guests turned in feigned awe to look at the baby in the crib. The baby stretched and smiled in his sleep as adult-sized gas escaped his baby-sized bowels.

"God bless him," said someone, breaking the tension. The laughter, the gossip, the flirting, and the complaining resumed, cuing the hired help that it was time to bring out the food. No one noticed that the twins were gone. Actually, no one had really noticed that they had been there in the first place.

CHAPTER 2

Teresa was content. No. Not exactly content—more like bored. Five years ago, she thought the world revolved around her baby. While it still did in many ways, he didn't need her quite as much anymore. She sighed as she watched Christopher playing happily on the swings with the other children visiting the park today.

She sat on a bench at one end of the park, feeling the warm summer breeze on her face. She shut her eyes, just a little annoyed at the bright sunshine that seemed to ignore her feelings. Just a few clouds interspersed here and there in the blue sky might reflect her mood a little better.

"Hey! I was on my way to the store and I saw you sittin' here. How ya doin?" Teresa's cousin Fanny sat down on the bench. The overpowering aroma of Fanny's perfume accented her arrival. Teresa imagined the impending embrace all in slow motion. First, the perfume. Then, the outstretched hands with perfectly manicured, long, fake nails reaching toward her. Eyes with long, fake eyelashes slowly closing, revealing elaborately gilded lids. The nose was next, pointed and aimed at Teresa's left ear. The outlined and heavily made-up mouth was not far behind, kissing the air first at the left side then at the right side of Teresa's face. Then, the mouth would open and stay open as a barrage of gossip, questions, and comments came flowing out. How did she do it without taking a breath? Teresa wondered if what she'd heard about circular breathing was true and if Fanny might have invented it.

Actually, Teresa sort of liked Fanny—in small doses. She could be very entertaining, or at least distracting, and that's exactly what she needed right now.

"I'm doing fine, Fanny," said Teresa, not really meaning it.

"Fine, shmine. You look like shit."

"Excuse me?"

"You heard me. I should maybe do your nails for ya or something." Gum snaps punctuated her sentences.

"Thanks, Fanny, but they would just get messed up. I can't have beautiful nails and play with play dough, ya know?"

"Oh, yeah. The miracle kid." Fanny laughed through her nose. "Ya like being a mother?"

"Of course I do! What a thing to ask! How could you ask that, Fanny?"

In the brief silence that followed, Teresa thought, I think I like being a mother. I used to like being a mother.

"What's the sigh for, then?" Fanny smiled knowingly. "Hey, look. I love my kids, too, baby, but sometimes ya just gotta get out and do somethin' for yourself. Ya know, to make yourself feel like somebody again."

"Well, I have been thinking about going back to work as soon as Christopher is in school. He starts kindergarten next month. Full day kindergarten. I could maybe get a part-time job or something."

"I think that's what you need to do, Teresa. Get a job. Meet new people. Make some grown-up friends. My god, I can't believe the miracle baby is five years old already. Geez!" She shook her head in amazement. "Anyways, I gotta go now, before the store is out of everything I need. See ya later, sweetie. Say hi to Joseph for me."

She enveloped Teresa in an odoriferous hug, slung her designer pocketbook over her shoulder, stood teetering on very pointed high-heeled shoes, and continued down the street toward her original destination. Teresa watched her go, just a little bit envious of her fascination-factor.

"Johnny, please be gentle!" Teresa's attention was suddenly diverted outward by the handsome boy vigorously pushing her son on the swing. "You know I've asked you that before. He's a lot younger than you and you can't push him so high. He might fall off or get scared."

"Sorry, Mrs. D'Antoni. I just forget sometimes." The crooked smile he gave her was charming. He made sure he was at the park everyday at this time so he could help Mrs. D'Antoni with Christopher. She was learning to trust him. Hopefully soon he could get a job babysitting for her or something so he could be around the kid more. How else could he do what he needed to do?

Johnny stopped the swing and put his head near Christopher's. "Sorry, little guy. Did that scare you? I won't push you so high this time. OK?"

"It didn't scare me, Johnny," grinned Christopher. "You can push me as high as you want to. I like it."

"I know you do, Christopher. But we have to obey Mommy, OK? She's the boss. There will be other times—later—for doing fun stuff that Mommy won't have to know about."

"I don't think so, Johnny." Where had Michael come from? Darn! "If Christopher doesn't tell his mother, I will. You shouldn't encourage him that way." Michael had a way of showing up at all the wrong times, in Johnny's opinion.

"I didn't mean we'd do anything terrible."

"Sure." Michael wasn't convinced. "Hi, Mrs. D'Antoni!" Michael waved at Christopher's mother.

"Oh, hello, Michael." Teresa hadn't seen him come onto the playground, but that wasn't unusual. He was quieter than his brother and much more reserved. He made her a little uncomfortable, but she couldn't exactly explain why. She had tried to once, when telling her husband about her day. Maybe it was the way his eyes looked right into hers or the way he spoke to her as if he was an adult instead of a child. He did smile occasionally, but mostly—always—he seemed to have something serious and important on his mind. Joseph thought she was crazy. He liked the curly-headed boy and had told Teresa to invite both boys over to play with Christopher since they had taken such an interest in him and were kind to him. She was not ready to do that just yet. For heaven's sake, she didn't even know their mother.

Teresa's smile started to slip a bit as she thought about that. What kind of mother sends her ten-year-old boys off to play in the park by themselves? She must be a lazy, heartless woman.

"Michael?"

"Yes, Mrs. D'Antoni?"

"Michael, where is your mother?" The words just popped out of Teresa's mouth. She thought for a moment that perhaps she shouldn't be so nosey. Perhaps she was being rude and she would make the boys angry. But Michael smiled and she felt better.

"Why do you want to know, Mrs. D'Antoni?"

"Umm. Well. Umm." She didn't think she should tell him she thought their mother was an awful parent, so she fudged a little. "Well, I was going to ask her if she would let you boys come to my house to play with Christopher."

Michael appeared to be pondering the invitation. Teresa felt she had to give a reason so she wouldn't appear weird or anything. Inviting ten-year-olds over to play with a five-year-old? What if the twins went home and told their mother she had just said that out of the blue? Their mom would think she was the weird one.

"I mean, I'm thinking of going to go back to work in a few months, and I could use the help with Christopher when he comes home from school. Like a babysitting job, but fun, because you and Johnny like playing with Christopher, right?" Oh god, Teresa, stop babbling! She was overdoing this a bit in her self-imposed embarrassment.

Johnny couldn't help the grin that spread across his face. Jackpot!

"Mrs. D'Antoni, I apologize for my brother's rudeness." Johnny playfully pushed Michael aside. "I would love to babysit for you anytime and would love to come to your house to help with Christopher. It's hard for a boy my age to earn much money and I'm trying to earn money for a computer." He turned to Christopher, who had followed him over to where Teresa was sitting. "That OK with you, buddy?"

"Oh yes! Mom, can Johnny and Michael really come over? That would be so, so, so, SO great!"

"So, I am always available, Mrs. D'Antoni, even though Michael may not be." Johnny stepped in front of Michael, edging him out of the way with a surreptitious, well-placed elbow. "And I would love to come. Just name the day."

"Thank you, Johnny." Teresa was relieved. "I don't have a job yet, but as soon as I do, I'll talk to my husband about having you come in the afternoons to help with Christopher. I'm sure he'll agree."

"Thanks, Mrs. D'Antoni. We've got to go now. It's getting late and we have…homework…to do. See you tomorrow!"

Johnny pulled Michael away and hurried down the path and out of the park. Teresa smiled again and took Christopher's hand. "Time to go home. Daddy will be there soon and I have to make dinner." Teresa and Christopher walked the short distance home in silence, both lost in thought. As they climbed the stairs onto the front porch,

Teresa realized that she still didn't know who the twins' mother was. Oh well. She would ask them again tomorrow.

"Homework?" Michael questioned Johnny as they walked together out of the park. "Why did you tell her that?"

"Why not? All kids have homework."

"We're not kids and I've never seen you do homework."

Johnny shrugged. "So what. This way she thinks I'm a good student and a responsible kid, yadda, yadda, yadda and we're in."

"You shouldn't lie."

Johnny laughed. "Well, it got us an invitation, didn't it?"

"Well, yes."

"No thanks to you, I might add. You stood there like an idiot, saying nothing. Good thing I am so quick on my feet. Good thing I am so charming. Good thing I am..."

"Stop it!" Michael interrupted. "Stop insulting me!"

Johnny shrugged. "Suit yourself. At least we'll be close to the kid."

"You are still not allowed to hurt him, you know."

"Yeah, so? I'll still win this. I'll still achieve the goal. Not you. Me." Johnny's arrogance was sickening.

"You can not hurt him," Michael repeated.

"I heard you," said Johnny, grinning. "No problem. There's more than one way to skin a cat. So to speak."

Michael sighed and the two boys disappeared into the dusk.

CHAPTER 3

Teresa fussed over Christopher and couldn't seem to stand still. She looked herself over in the big mirror hanging over the fireplace. Trim, neat, and dressed very fashionably. Not a hair out of place. She ran her hands over her hair anyway. Why was she nervous? Christopher would be in the spotlight, not her. First Communion was a big deal in this family and she wanted everything to be perfect. She wanted her husband's approval. She wanted her mother-in-law's and father-in-law's approval. And the cousins. And the family friends. And the priest. Especially the priest! She brushed imaginary lint from Christopher's small white suit and ran her hand over his hair to try and tame the stray cowlick in the back. The limo would be here soon and she needed to have everything ready. Joseph hated being late.

Christopher wriggled in annoyance. He wanted to go play. Even at the ripe old age of seven, he did not know what the big deal was about eating a cracker and drinking wine. He was curious to see, though, if it actually turned into Jesus' body and blood. He thought maybe the priest switched the cracker out for chicken when no one was looking. No one would actually eat another person's body. That would be gross.

His father had hired a magician for his seventh birthday party this year and he did swap-out tricks like that, only nobody ate any of them. Johnny and Michael had come to the party and Johnny had explained that the tricks were just tricks—not real. He had even showed Christopher how to make a coin disappear by hiding it in his opposite hand. That was very cool and made him feel important because he knew something the other kids his age did not know. Kind of like Santa Claus. That was just a story to get kids to behave around Christmas time. He knew Santa wasn't real. Christopher was very skeptical that this Communion thing would be anything but a magic trick and that Jesus was anything but a story to make people do things the priest wanted them to do, like give up their money.

Christopher put his hand in his pants pocket and felt for the two silver dollars he had hidden there. They jingled quietly, reassuring him of their presence. There was no way he was giving these up to any old priest. His grandfather had given them to him to offer the priest during confession, which he was supposed to do in penance for his sins before he could take communion today. Penance. Sins. What was that anyway? Big words he had learned in his classes that meant absolutely nothing to him. The best he could figure was that he had to pay for the food the priest was going to magically make appear and part of the conjuring spell was to say the words, "I have sinned."

Michael told him that sinning was doing something wrong. What would happen if he kept the silver dollars? Was that doing something wrong if he swapped them out with a couple of shiny pennies he had in his bank? If the priest could swap crackers and chicken, then certainly he could swap silver dollars and pennies. Christopher really liked the silver dollars. He should not have to give them to a wrinkly old priest.

"Hey! My big boy!" Christopher's father walked into the room. He was flushed with excitement. He gave his wife a brief kiss and then turned his attention to his son. "Are you ready?"

Christopher spun around in a circle with his hands out, palms up. "Yep!"

"You are sure handsome today in your suit!" His mother's cousin Fanny walked into the room and gave Christopher a pinch on the cheek with her knuckles, taking care to keep her long fingernails from scratching him. "God bless him!"

Christopher rubbed his cheek. "Hi Fanny. Did you bring me a present?"

Christopher's mother gave a small gasp at his rudeness but Fanny just laughed. "I sure did, honey, but you can't have it until the party. I'm headed out now to pick up Nonno and Momma and will meet you at the church."

Fanny's perfume was strong and her makeup a little much for going to church. She looked a bit like a clown, though, with the blue stuff on her eyes and the bright red lipstick, so maybe that was appropriate for a first Communion. Magic and clowns. This might be fun after all!

Teresa and Joseph took Christopher's hands and led him out to the limo waiting outside the front door. They climbed into the back, waved to Fanny, and signaled the chauffeur to head for the church.

When they arrived, the priest met them at the door and led them to one of the two confessionals along one side of the church.

"Go ahead, Christopher. We'll be right here," said his mother.

Joseph leaned down and whispered, "Remember what you were told to do?" Christopher nodded.

As the priest talked to his parents, he climbed up the small step into one side of the confessional. It was dark. He was a little scared. His knee bumped something soft and warm. A hand reached out and clamped over his mouth so he could not cry out. In the next few seconds as his eyes adjusted, he went from being frightened to wanting to laugh with joy. It was Johnny!

"How did you…"

Johnny again put a hand over Christopher's mouth and a finger up against his own lips and whispered, "Sshhh! I'm not supposed to be here but I thought you might want a friend nearby so it's not so scary."

"This is so cool! Thanks! But what if the priest…"

"He won't notice me. I promise! I'll help you remember what you are supposed to say and do."

"Thanks Johnny. You're the best!" Christopher thought for a minute then added, "Do I have to give the priest my money?"

Johnny laughed quietly. "No way, buddy. You keep your money."

There was a rustling on the other side of the confessional as the priest entered the booth. Johnny put his finger to his mouth and winked.

There wasn't much to confess. Christopher had always done what his parents told him to do, even if he didn't want to. They loved him so much—how could he disappoint them? He intended to keep the coins in his pocket, but how could he confess that? If the priest knew, he would make him give them up. So, he could confess to a lie then. He would lie. Johnny nodded his head slightly—almost as if he could read Christopher's mind and was giving approval.

The priest told Christopher to be careful how he behaved because breaking any of the commandments, whether it was lying or killing, would place his soul in danger of going to Hell. It was important for him to be really, truly sorry and come regularly to confession because a soul cannot enter Heaven with unforgiven sins.

The priest seemed happy to be done with the confession part and encouraged Christopher to visit him often in the private booth. Johnny rolled his eyes, and Christopher giggled.

Teresa scooped him up in a hug as he came out of the confessional. She did not notice his right hand in his pocket palming the coins. She gave him a kiss on both cheeks. "What's so funny, little man?" she asked.

"Nothing," Christopher replied, thankful he'd already confessed to lying. He figured he was covered for the day at least. He wasn't sure what a soul was but Hell sounded awful.

Teresa put him down and took his hand. Christopher saw his father slip the priest a $100 bill before taking his other hand and leading them all toward the front of the church. His coins were safe! And his. Only his.

They were the first to arrive for the special Mass but Christopher knew exactly where to sit. They had practiced it as a class this past week. He tugged his hands free and skipped over to his place in the front row pew. He looked back and saw that his parents were very proud of him. It was obvious by the smiles on their faces and the way his mother had her hands folded over her heart. His father's arm was draped over his mother's shoulders and they stood for a few seconds longer than they normally would have, just looking at him. As others started coming in, they took their seats not too far away and near the aisle so they could get good pictures of him. He wasn't embarrassed, though. He enjoyed the attention.

The altar was covered with fragrant flowers that were going to make him sneeze anytime now. He held it in for as long as he could, then ducked his head under the pew and covered his mouth tightly so that it only came out as a little squeak instead of an "achoo" that would have echoed through the ornate wooden interior of the church.

While he had his head down, he could see the shoes of everyone sitting behind him for at least a dozen rows.

Wait! He recognized those sneakers! Christopher popped up and turned around. Yes! They were here! They both came after all!

Johnny and Michael waved. Michael's wave was composed and respectful of the occasion. Johnny, however, grinned broadly and raised both hands, waving them back and forth with more energy than appropriate. He mouthed the words, "Hey Christopher! You're doing great!"

Christopher grinned back before turning around to face the front as the priest began walking toward the altar, the incense swinging in front of him.

The sermon was directed at the row of seven- and eight-year-olds sitting in the front pew and made absolutely no sense to Christopher, but that didn't matter. Soon it was time for them to file up in a single line to receive their first Communion. Christopher opened his mouth for the cracker. Yuck! It tasted like cardboard. He almost said so, but caught himself just in time. It was definitely NOT chicken. The wine was next, and at least it tasted decent. He wondered how the priest could get away with having everyone drink from the same cup, though. Didn't he know about germs? His parents had always been very careful to teach him to avoid germs. He guessed it was part of the magic trick.

When he was back at his seat, and while he waited for the others to receive their Communion, Christopher bit his wrist so hard it bled. It hurt but it didn't taste anything like the bread the priest gave him. And the blood tasted a bit metallic—nothing at all like the wine. Either the priest lied about this being the body and blood of Christ (and therefore lying wasn't a mortal sin) or the magic trick didn't work this time.

Disappointing. Very disappointing.

CHAPTER 4

M ichael sat at the kitchen table with Christopher on his left. They sat side by side and could both see through the sliding glass doors to the woodsy backyard. It was a beautiful May afternoon. The sun was shining, the birds were singing. A squirrel was perched on the deck railing gazing in at them and snacking on an acorn. Michael would love to be outside among them. Instead, he sighed and turned back to Christopher.

"The variable is the x or y. It's the number you don't know," he explained patiently.

Christopher's eyes squinted in concentration. Eighth grade was so hard! He hated it. His left elbow pressed against the corner of the paper as he supported his head with his left hand and bounced the eraser end of his pencil on the table over and over again with his right hand.

"I get that part. But is there an easier way to figure it out? Like, when the teacher showed us x + 2 = 4, I could guess that x is two. But the problems she gave us for homework are much harder. Look: 35 + x + 6x = 0. Zero. Nothing. What equals nothing? Why do I even care if it equals nothing? Isn't that like saying it's worth nothing? When I have something that's worth nothing, I throw it away. I'd like to throw this problem away!" Christopher angrily crumpled up the paper and tossed it toward the garbage can. It missed and landed among the other dozen or so crumpled papers that were lying on the floor.

Michael patiently put another paper in front of him. "It's not that bad, Christopher. I can explain it to you."

Christopher sat slumped over, his head and hands resting flat on the table. He opened the eye that wasn't pressed against his hands and watched as Michael began writing the problem and explaining how like terms could be combined and how to subtract from each side, then divide, and presto! Like magic, an answer appeared. Christopher sighed. "It looks easy when you do it."

"Here's another problem. You try. Take it step by step. I'll remind you of what to do if you get stuck and before you know it, you'll be able to do everything by yourself!"

Christopher picked up his head, then the pencil, and began slowly copying the numbers. "Michael, when you were in eighth grade, did you have trouble with math?"

"Well, I've always been pretty good at figuring things out."

"You are so lucky to be a senior in high school, Michael. I can't wait until next year when I'll be in high school."

"Why is that?"

"I think people stop teasing you in high school."

"People are teasing you?"

"Yeah." Christopher said reluctantly. "Just a little bit." He turned his head so that Michael could see the left side of his face. "I think I gave him a reminder of me, too, though."

Michael winced. "Ouch. That looks like it hurt." The bruise under Christopher's eye was turning purple-yellow. "What happened?"

"There's these guys at school that say I'm a pansy and a pretty-boy. They've pretty much bothered me since sixth grade. I just finally had enough so I told them to go f themselves. They told me they would rather do that to me since I was such a pretty boy." Christopher paused, looking warily at Michael, wondering if he should tell the rest of the story.

"And?"

"And…I ran." Christopher shrugged. "They caught up to me just as I got to Nonno's house. I got a few hits in. They got a few hits in. Then Nonno came out and told them he would have all of them killed if they didn't leave me alone. So, they left. Everyone is afraid of Nonno."

"Wow, kid. I'm sorry I wasn't there for you."

"It's OK Michael, I know you have your own life."

"Yeah, but I should have been there for you."

"It's really OK. Johnny showed up right afterwards anyway and he and Nonno
had a talk about what to do."

"Mmm…" Michael seemed deep in thought.

"Really, it's OK," Christopher repeated. "I don't think they'll bother me again. They'll probably just move on to hassle another poor kid. Hey, Michael, did anything like that ever happen to you?"

"Hmm? Oh, sorry. I was just thinking." Michael smiled at Christopher. "Yes, actually. I've had similar things happen to me. I've been in a few fights."

"Really? What did you do?"

"I prayed."

"Prayed? How did that help?"

"Well, other…that is, others came to fight with me and we were able to beat back the bad guys."

"Oh, that is so cool!" Christopher was impressed. "Did you get into trouble with your parents?"

The sliding glass doors opened and a cheerful, tousled head popped around the corner.

"Hey you two! Starting homework without me?" Johnny came in and slid the door shut behind him.

"Hi, Johnny. We were actually talking about that fight I had last week. I can't believe you didn't tell Michael about it."

"Well, kiddo, I thought you might want to keep it somewhat quiet. You did run, ya know. We can't let it get out there that you're a scaredy-cat, can we?" He winked at Christopher.

"Johnny, stop teasing him. He did OK and you know it."

"Yeah, I know it, brother, because I was there. Where were you?" The smile wasn't exactly friendly anymore. It was almost triumphal, in a way.

"Knock it off, you two." Teresa came into the kitchen carrying a bag of groceries. "There will be no arguing in this house." Her smile took the edge off the words. "There, will, however, be lots of helping. So, the three of you can help me bring in the groceries, then I will make you all a snack."

Christopher and Michael jumped to their feet and followed Johnny out of the door and to the car. Teresa hummed cheerfully to herself as she took the bags from the boys and began putting the groceries away. Over the past eight years the twins had become an important part of her life and a welcome addition to her "family". She smiled sheepishly to herself as she remembered her earlier trepidation about inviting them to her house. They had been a godsend, really. Her sisters and brothers all had large families. Johnny and Michael gave her household the same feeling—a large, loving family. She just couldn't feel luckier. She would ask them to stay for dinner again tonight. Their family didn't seem to mind. Johnny had told her they came from a very, very large family and were never missed since there were so many others for the father to look after. Johnny also said he had no mother and that his father was actually grateful that Teresa took an interest in them and encouraged them to help her out whenever they could. Poor boys. No mother and an overworked and overwhelmed father.

The boys came back into the kitchen carrying the rest of the groceries. "Here ya go, Mom." She just loved that they all called her "Mom."

"Thanks boys," she said, handing them each a sliced apple with a scoop of peanut butter. "Now, Christopher, please finish your homework while I get dinner ready. Johnny and

Michael, you can stay for dinner?" It was more a statement than a question, but they both nodded.

"Thank you, we would love to," Johnny replied for both of them.

Teresa took out her pots and pans and sauce and pasta and was very, very happy.

CHAPTER 5

Deja vu.

At least that's how it felt as Christopher walked to the front of the church and sat with the other confirmation candidates. They were the same group of kids that he had sat with seven years ago for his first Communion. Now they were all finishing eighth grade together and, as obedient Catholics, were doing what the church required them to do.

Christopher wasn't sure he wanted to be here, but it was expected of him so, like the outwardly compliant person he was, he put a smile on his face and sat down. After this, he wouldn't have to come to church anymore—except for Christmas and Easter—just like his dad. Nonno and Momma were different. They came every week without fail. Christopher didn't think that was because they were particularly religious, though. It was more a control thing. Nonno kept tabs on the priests and they did his bidding in the community. Nothing like the fear of Hell to keep your goonies in line! Hell didn't scare him, though. It was just as make-believe as bread becoming flesh or wine becoming blood. Geez. How could grown people actually fall for this?

Today he was supposed to confirm his faith in God and in the holy Catholic church. But he had no faith in either. This was simply a ritual he must get through in order to stop coming to church. Christopher shook his head and looked down at the new Bible on his lap. His parents had given it to him this morning to commemorate the day. It was soft black leather with his name printed in gold on the front cover. Inside, his parents, well his mom really, had written, "We are proud of you on your confirmation day. May God always lead you in the way you should go. Proverbs 4:11."

He didn't know what had gotten into his mom lately. She seemed very keen on God and reading the Bible and religious stuff like that. It annoyed his dad a little but Christopher and his father had bonded by teasing his mom about it. She just smiled good-naturedly when they did that and said, "You'll see. You'll see I'm right. One day..."

The only difference about today that kept this from being a true deja vu was that neither Johnny nor Michael came. He had wanted one of them to be his sponsor but they couldn't because they weren't Catholic. Instead, Fanny's no-good-husband Jack (at least that's what his father called him) was here to do the honors. He owed Nonno a favor so here he was. Christopher suspected that Johnny and Michael knew this was just a farce for him. He imagined Johnny's grin and Michael's worried frown. But he was fine. Just this one last step and then—freedom!

Christopher looked up as the bishop walked by. It would be hard to miss him. He was dressed in elaborately embroidered red vestments. The hat—well, it was ridiculous in Christopher's opinion. The bishop droned on and on, giving a sermon that would soon be forgotten by everyone in attendance. Who really listened anyway? The questions asked and answered by the confirmands were rote with no meaning—by any of them, Christopher noticed. So he wasn't the only one feeling this way! One of the other boys was stifling a yawn. Another shuffled his feet. A third was staring out the window. A girl passed a note to a friend sitting next to her. Wow, was she cute! She stuck the tip of her tongue out at Christopher and crossed her eyes. Yikes! OK, back off of that one!

When his turn for confirmation came, Christopher stood up and walked forward with his sponsor. "Hey, bud," whispered Jack. "Important day, huh?"

"Yeah. Sure," replied Christopher.

Jack put his hand on Christopher's shoulder and said his new name, Francis. Francis was the patron saint of Italy and therefore important enough to be his confirmation name, according to Nonno. He would be Christopher Francis D'Antoni.

The bishop dipped his finger in the holy oil. He touched Christopher on the forehead, dragging his oily finger down and then across, making the shape of a cross. "Francis, be sealed with the gift of the Holy Spirit."

"Amen," said Christopher dutifully.

"Peace be with you."

"And also with you."

A priest gave him the bread and wine. Nothing. No magic. No lightning bolt. Nothing.

"May the blessing of the almighty God the Father, God the Son, and God the Holy Spirit come upon you and stay with you forever."

"Amen."

It was done.

CHAPTER 6

Christopher sat nervously at the kitchen table, his book bag packed and clutched tightly in front of him. He tried not to be so nervous but this was a big deal. It was the first day of high school and not just any high school—the premiere private high school on the east coast that only the very best could afford to get into. Sure, a couple poor kids probably got scholarships, but not him. His family was pretty well off, thanks to Nonno's businesses.

He should be happy, but he just felt queasy. He was sure everyone there would be smarter and have less acne than he did. He woke up this morning with one huge zit on his nose. Today, of all days! Well, they wouldn't be calling him "pretty boy" with this glaring blemish. So, maybe he wouldn't get beaten up on the first day. Maybe he would just get teased and made fun of for his zit. He wondered if it was possible to be absent from this school on the first day without penalty. His Mom would write him a note—he was sure he could get her to do that. If only she would come downstairs before his father. His father would never allow that. His father would drag him by the ear into school and demand to know if there was anyone who dared—dared—make fun of his boy.

The clock in living room chimed seven times. Christopher heard the stairs creak and two sets of footsteps coming. Teresa and Joseph came into the kitchen together.

"Good morning, Christopher." His mom gave him a kiss on the top of his head as she walked by.

"How's the high-schooler?" His dad patted him on the back and sat down in the chair next to him, reaching for the newspaper. "Teresa, my coffee!" Joseph lightly tapped his cup on the table.

"Well, Dad, I'm not feeling so well."

Teresa filled Joseph's cup with coffee, then her own. She sat down, picked up the cup of steaming hot coffee between her hands, sipping it and gazing over the cup at Christopher. After a moment she said, "Christopher, it's normal to be a little nervous on your first day. You'll do fine."

Christopher slumped down in his chair.

"Really, Christopher," Teresa continued. "This is a whole new set of people. You'll make friends quickly, I'm sure."

When Christopher didn't answer, Teresa's wide-eyed gaze at her husband implored him to say something comforting to their son. Joseph sighed and put down the newspaper.

"Look, son. If you go in acting like a pansy, they'll call you a pansy. If you walk in with your head down trying to hide that zit on your face…" Christopher's hand flew up and covered his nose. "…then they'll make fun of it. Go in with your head held high, like a real man, and they'll treat you with respect. Stop being such a cry-baby about it, for god's sake. It's just high school."

"Joseph!" This was not exactly the speech Teresa had in mind. "Stop it! He needs your support, not your criticism."

"And you baby him, Teresa. Let him grow up. It's time he stopped being such a momma's-boy."

"And it's time you stopped being so hard on him. All the time finding fault."

"I couldn't find the faults if they wasn't there, Teresa."

"You are horrible this morning. What's gotten into you? Drink your coffee. Maybe you need the caffeine. Maybe you'll lighten up after you've had your fix."

"Shut up. I don't need to listen to you yappin' at me first thing in the morning."

"No, what you need is some food so you'll stop being so crabby." Teresa opened the refrigerator door and reached for the eggs. "Christopher? You want some eggs?"

Christopher stood up, slung his book bag over one shoulder and walked to the front door. "No thanks, Ma. I'm going now."

"Get back here and eat your breakfast!" growled Joseph.

"Have a nice day, Christopher," said Teresa blowing him a kiss as he walked out the door, slamming it behind him.

It was under a mile walk to school—0.622 miles to be exact. Christopher shuffled along, killing time by kicking pebbles, tying a shoe, sitting on a park bench—anything to postpone the inevitable. He was lucky the private school was so close. At least, that's what his parents had assured him. He wasn't so sure he was lucky at anything. So far, his life had pretty much sucked. At least at school it did. He couldn't help being handsome. Yet the kids teased him about that. And now he couldn't help having a zit on his nose. He was absolutely sure he would be made fun of for that. He couldn't help being an only child in a culture of big families. He couldn't help being a member of the D'Antoni mob family. He couldn't help a lot of things, come to think of it. Life was pretty much out of his control. He just lived day by day, by day, by day, by day…

"Hey, Christopher!" A horn beeped out a noisy greeting as a bright yellow Corvette convertible, top down, pulled up beside him. "Need a ride?"

"Johnny!" Christopher immediately felt lighter, happier, better. "Where are you going?" He threw his back pack into the back seat and climbed in. "Take me with you?"

Johnny laughed. "OK, but I think you should know I'm on my way to your school."

"Uggh." Christopher's smile disappeared. "Why would you want to do that?"

"Well, I'm a volunteer coach and will be helping out in PE classes and coaching this fall."

"Yeah?" Maybe this wouldn't be so bad after all.

"When did you get that gig?" Christopher asked.

"Just yesterday," Johnny said. "They had an unexpected opening when one of the PE teachers broke his hip last night. They remembered my glorious performances on Sleepy

Hollow's high school sports teams last year and called to ask if I would be interested in coaching. Like—of course! How could I turn down the opportunity to be there for my little brother?"

"You took this job to be with me? To help me out?"

"You got that right, kiddo. I thought you might need some help—behind the scenes, of course." Johnny watched Christopher nod thoughtfully. "I'll get you off on the right foot, then you're on your own."

"Thanks, Johnny." Christopher relaxed. It would be nice to have the support.

"What are you coaching?"

"Fencing."

"Fencing?"

"Yeah. It's fighting with a sword."

"I knew that—I just didn't know you fenced."

"There's a lot you don't know about me, brother."

"But I've known you since I was a little kid."

"Yeah, but we haven't really shared anything as equals—you were the little kid and I was your babysitter-slash-older brother. There were just some things it wasn't appropriate to do together."

"But I'm older now."

"Yep. You are." Johnny grinned. "Now, we can do things together."

Christopher sat up straighter and grinned back. "I'm tired of being the goody-two-shoes pretty boy who gets picked on all the time! So I want to do it all—appropriate or not."

"No problem. I'll be the kind of friend who shows you how." Johnny winked. "Just to be sure you're safe and all."

"Right. Safe—but fun." Christopher couldn't stop smiling. It looked like his luck was about to change.

"Here we are." Johnny turned the convertible onto the drive leading into the 137-acre campus. An old but well-kept stone building sat at the top of the hill. Featured prominently over the large wooden entryway to the campus was the motto in Latin, "Excellence in Academics, Excellence in Life."

Johnny drove slowly up the drive to the main building. Students were gathered on the lawn in small groups, clutching their new textbooks and getting caught up on all of the gossip from the summer. Johnny smiled and winked at the pretty girls who stopped to stare and giggle with their friends as he drove by. Christopher was happy to be in this car at this moment with this friend. He copied the self-assured smirk he saw on Johnny's face and nodded coolly at a brown-haired cheerleader-type as they passed by. She smiled and waved back at him, tossing her hair flirtatiously. This was a good start. A very good start to high school.

Johnny smiled too, but for quite different reasons. He looped slowly around the driveway again, basking in the attention of the students—both male and female. The boys swooned over his car. The girls swooned over him. Finally, he stopped in front of an imposing stone building with a large number 2 over the door and turned to Christopher.

"Here ya go, kiddo. Your classes await you."

"Thanks, Johnny." Christopher did not reach for the door handle.

"You'll be fine!"

"I hope so."

"You will. You'll see. Just keep that confident smile on your face I saw a few minutes ago and you'll do great. You're certainly smart enough to get the high grades. And I'll help you with the girl stuff."

"Thanks. OK. Here goes." He reached for the door handle and stopped short. "Any chance that you can pick me up at 2:00?"

"No problem, bro. I'll pick you up right here. You can come with me to fencing practice if you want to."

"Sure. Thanks. See ya later." With a deep breath, Christopher finally got out of the car and walked into building #2. He glanced down at his schedule even though he didn't really need to since he'd memorized it weeks before. Building #2, room #2. Biology. Simple.

He looked up and there it was. Room #2. And there he was. The bully who had given him a black eye last year was going into room #2 with an arm slung casually over the shoulders of the brown-haired girl he had just waved to on the way in.

The girl was smiling, and he heard her say, "Oh, Billy, you know I can't do that!" followed by a giggle. Billy looked around to make sure he had an audience before mimicking her breathless tone, "Oh Crystal, you know you can't resist my charm forever. You'll do it and beg me for more." They disappeared into the classroom, but Christopher heard her giggle through the open doorway.

"Move butthead."

"In or out, idiot."

"You're blocking the doorway, geek."

Those were the nicer things said as the other students tried to get around Christopher and into room #2. He was paralyzed, not knowing what he should do. Go in and be humiliated by the bully Billy and his pretty girlfriend. Or stay out and cut his first class of high school, which would definitely anger his father and mother. He'd pay either way. He started to back up and turn around. He wanted to go the opposite way. But he heard Johnny's voice in his head saying, "Keep that confident smile and you'll do great," so he gathered together all the courage he had and walked into room #2, a smile—hopefully a confident one—frozen into place.

Not one person looked at him. Not one head turned to see what his decision had been. Not one insult was hurled his way. They were all busy talking to one another about their summer, their newest conquest, their first football game. Christopher found an empty desk on the right side of the room near a window and sat down. A skinny, pimply-faced boy with thick glasses at the desk in front of him turned around and stared at him.

"Hi." Christopher thought he'd try a friendly approach first.

"Hi," the boy replied, still not smiling.

"I'm Christopher."

"Yeah. I know. The miracle boy. You don't recognize me, do you?"

"No. Should I?"

"Your Mom is cousins with my mom's second husband Pete."

"Oh."

"I met you at a family picnic about four years ago when we were about ten years old I think. Then my mom split with Pete so we didn't go to no more picnics at your house. My name's Tony."

"I think I remember you."

"Yeah. It's OK. I know ya don't. I ain't that memorable. You, though, you was all my Mom talked about. The miracle child. Like you was Christ hisself. She says that's why they named you Christopher, 'cause it sounded like Christ. Your ma couldn't have kids, and somehow she ended up with you."

"Well, I know that's the story they tell, but it's just a family story. Very exaggerated."

"Hell, I know ya ain't perfect. I saw ya steal a thumb drive from Walmarts this summer. It was slick how you slipped it out of the package and put the empty package back on the shelf. Cool. Very cool. I tried to do that once but got caught. I ain't got the innocent look you got. Nobody'd bother you none. Hey! Maybe you could teach me how you do it. What do ya think? We could be partners. You swipe the merch. I got someone who'd buy it from us. We'd make some good money."

"I didn't really steal it. I just forgot to pay, that's all." Christopher was embarrassed and a little angry. He was not used to being caught. He enjoyed being thought of as the perfect child and was more than a little upset that there was a person who knew the truth.

"I won't tell anyone about it. Promise! I was just hoping we could like, you know, hang out or something."

"Well, sure, yeah, sometime. We'll hang out sometime."

Tony finally grinned, revealing a full set of shiny braces. "Great. That'd be great. Me and the miracle boy—friends."

The teacher walked into the room and cleared her throat. Tony gave a short nod and turned back to the front. Christopher slid down in his chair and sighed with relief as the teacher began the lesson. So far, unnoticed. Good. Very good.

CHAPTER 7

T he day went by more quickly than Christopher thought it would. Only two more periods to go. He actually enjoyed his classes, especially those where he could sit in the back of the room and that had teachers that didn't expect students to participate, like this English class. The teacher just lectured and he just took notes. Most of the students dozed or drew pictures or texted their friends. Christopher watched them, getting the "lay of the land" as he listened to the teacher drone on and on. Who was top dog? Who were the jocks? Who were the nerds? Which girl had hooked up with which boy?

Christopher sighed as he gazed at Crystal, sitting toward the front of the room near the door and next to the wall, passing notes back and forth with Billy. Billy was sitting next to her and slowly moved his desk closer and closer until they were only about eighteen inches apart. He pretended to yawn, covering his mouth with his left hand and stretching his right arm out, palm back, so that his hand covered—and then touched—Crystal's breast.

She pushed it away, embarrassed. "Stop!" she whispered.

"But you know you want it," Billy whispered back.

Crystal looked like she might cry. She tried to move her desk away without calling any attention to herself, but the wall was too close. There was nowhere for her to go. The bell rang and she jumped up, knocking her books to the floor. Billy laughed and headed for the door. "Meet me out front after school," he demanded. "We'll go to my house for some privacy."

Once Billy was through the door, Christopher quietly moved across the room and helped Crystal pick up her books. She kept her head turned away, but Christopher could see that she was still trying not to cry.

"Hey," Christopher said.

"Hey," she replied.

Encouraged, Christopher continued. "I have study hall next. It's my last class for the day. We can sit outside and talk if you'd like to…"

"Oh, no, I couldn't." Crystal looked almost terrified. "If Billy were to find out…"

"What? What would he do to you?"

"Nothing! I shouldn't have said that."

"He beat me up last year." Christopher didn't know why he had confided that. It just came out of his mouth like a million other dumb things he had said in his 15 years. Embarrassed, Christopher continued, "I don't like the way he treated me, and I don't like the way he is treating you. He's a bully and a jerk."

Crystal was silent. She finished gathering her books and started for the door.

"Look, I'm sorry I said anything," Christopher tried to explain. "But he is a jerk, and you deserve better."

She paused and then said sarcastically, "Like you?"

Before Christopher could reply, Crystal was out the door and out of sight. He sighed and mumbled to himself, "I sure botched that one. Like everything else in my life. Now she thinks I'm a jerk too." Christopher shrugged. Maybe Johnny could help him fix this. He would talk to him on the way to fencing practice. Hey! Maybe he would join the fencing team! That might get him some points with the girls…with Crystal.

Pausing just another few seconds to be sure Billy was not waiting outside the door, Christopher took a deep breath and stepped out into the hallway. No one here. Good. He continued down the hallway and turned the corner.

Oh shit! Billy was waiting for him, with two of his friends on either side.

"Hey, dirt bag. Didn't get enough last year? You obviously want more of this…" Billy pounded his right fist into his left palm.

"No…no…" Christopher stammered and backed up. He looked around for help. No one here. Not good.

"Yes, you obviously do. You was flirting with my girl. I'll take care of her later, but now it's your turn. And your old grandpa is not here to help you now, pretty boy."

Billy's friends sneered and balled up their fists at their sides, making sure to position themselves so Christopher could see that. They all took a step toward him. Christopher looked frantically back and forth. No escape! He was trapped. He tried to put that smug, confident smile on his face that Johnny had encouraged, but it came out more like the smile of a stroke victim—scared and paralyzed.

As Christopher visualized Billy's fist coming toward his face in slow motion, knocking out all of his perfectly straight white teeth, Michael appeared behind them. He was tall—at least 6 feet 2 inches—but he seemed suddenly taller at this moment. Christopher hadn't seen him since middle school graduation and hadn't really missed him since Johnny had been around all summer. But now... now he was very, very happy to see him.

"Michael! Good to see you bro." Christopher put up a hand and gave an energetic wave. He kept his other hand defensively in front of his chest, palm out, as if he could somehow use the air to push Billy away.

"Hello. Is everything all right?" Michael asked.

"Yeah, everything is hunky dory. Me and my friend Christopher here was just having a conversation." Billy draped his arm across Christopher's shoulders. "Right, buddy?"

"Uh, right." Christopher didn't want to make things worse by tattling.

"Great," said Michael. "I could use some help in the shop if you guys have some free time."

"Nah, we gotta go," said Billy. As he and his friends started to walk away, Billy turned back to Christopher. "Later, friend," he sneered.

That sure sounded like a threat to Christopher. He hurried across the hall to walk beside Michael.

"Wow. Did you show up at just the right moment!" Christopher told him.

Michael smiled. "Glad to help."

"What are you doing here?"

"I'm a guest artist in the woodworking shop. I spent the summer studying with a carpenter, and I volunteered to share some of that knowledge with the students at this school. They took me up on my offer."

"I'm definitely adding that class to my schedule!"

"Already done, my man. I talked to your Mom this morning and she called the guidance office here to arrange it. It replaces your study hall this period. Somehow I knew you'd like it." Michael grinned. "Come on, I think your class starts in five minutes."

They walked together to the shop, Christopher's step much lighter now. BOTH Johnny and Michael here. This was great. Now if he could just get rid of Billy, high school might not be that bad.

CHAPTER 8

Johnny picked him up promptly at 2:00, just as he'd promised. Christopher was excited to tell him the news of the day.

"Oh man, you'll never believe what happened! I met this girl, Crystal. She's gorgeous!" Christopher exaggerated each syllable and threw in an extra one for good measure, pronouncing it gor-ge-ous.

"Unfortunately, she's Billy's girlfriend and he got mad. He cornered me in the hall and was going to beat me up, but Michael came just in time. Oh, geez. I think he might hurt Crystal. Billy, that is. Not Michael." Christopher's face showed horror at the thought and he turned a panicked look toward Johnny.

"Michael's here?" Johnny asked, barely hiding the anger behind his question.

"Yes, isn't that great?" Christopher said. "Didn't you know? I thought twins shared everything. Did you guys have an argument or something?"

"Of course I knew he was coming back. I just forgot," Johnny lied. "I'll catch up with him later. Now what's this about, hmm, was her name Crystal?"

"Crystal. Yes. Billy threatened her because she talked to me. He was super jealous. What should I do?"

"You want to be her knight in shining armor?" Johnny grinned. "I get it. Rescue the princess and she will fall in love with you, right?"

Christopher rolled his eyes. "Something like that. But seriously, should I warn her or something?"

"We can check up on her later—drive by her house after practice, OK?"

"OK," Christopher said. "That'd be great. Thanks."

They pulled into the parking lot in front of the huge gymnasium. The large, curved, dome-like roof was impressive, showing off the school colors—gold with black trim. The school's mascot, an enormous eagle, was painted on the side of the building. It was done with such skill that it almost looked real. The wings appeared to flutter as the sunlight reflected on the walls and the heat waves moved in the air around the building.

"Come on," Johnny told Christopher, taking the bag of practice swords from the backseat and slinging it over his shoulder. "You can either watch practice or participate. It's up to you. Tryouts will be next week. This week is just to teach the fundamentals of sword play so we have a chance of putting together a decent team. Anyone can come."

"Hey Christopher!" yelled a voice from across the parking lot. Oh, geez. It was Tony—from biology class. He was grinning from ear to ear, his braces shiny and prominent.

"That's Tony—he's somehow related to my mom— cousins or someone married to cousins or something. I don't really know. He thinks we're friends just because I said hello to him in biology class this morning," Christopher told Johnny. "He's kind of weird."

Johnny smiled. They walked toward Tony.

"Hi Tony," said Johnny. "Christopher told me about you. You interested in fencing?"

"Heck, yeah," Tony said still grinning. "Us skinny guys need some kind of defense, ya know?"

"Ah, um, well, it's a sport, not a way to hurt people," said Christopher. "Right, Johnny?"

"It is a sport, but it's also a way to fight—if you need to. Many of the old wars were fought with swords."

"I know that," said Christopher. "But now, in this century, people don't fight with swords for real." He paused. "Well, at least not in this country, right?"

Johnny grinned. "Correct. People don't fight with swords for real in this country." He led the boys into the gymnasium. About a dozen other students were waiting there. Christopher was surprised to see Crystal among them. He glanced at her and saw her wiggle her fingers in a quick, timid wave. She seemed surprised to see him too, and a little nervous. She kept looking around as if Billy might appear and force her to leave.

"All right, everyone. Come line up so we can get started." Johnny sounded very authoritative, very teacher-like. The students responded immediately, eager to begin.

Johnny handed out wooden swords. "These are your practice swords. We start with wooden swords so no one gets hurt. You'll get face masks and chest protectors later this week. We are only practicing moves today, not sparring, so you won't need a mask today. If you make the team, you will get the rest of the equipment you need because we will be using actual swords, called foils.

"Spread yourselves out so there is at least six feet of space all around you. More, if you can." The students complied.

Christopher held on to his wooden sword tightly with both hands, not moving. Tony swung his sword wildly around in a circle. Crystal looked like she was praying, her eyes tightly shut, thrusting upward with the sword perpendicular to the floor and held in both hands at eye level. Christopher wondered what she was thinking. If it were him, he would be imagining Billy receiving the tip of a sharp—definitely not wooden—sword. Even though he had told Tony swords were not for fighting, his imagination believed they could be very useful against bullies.

Johnny taught them how to hold the sword and demonstrated several stances they would use in competition. He also went over some thrusting moves that Christopher thought were super cool. By the end of practice, Christopher found he was sweating and his muscles were sore. Fencing was not easy, but, to his surprise, he liked it a lot. At least, he liked the parts of it so far where they didn't actually have to face an opponent.

"That's it for today. You all did great! If you are still interested, come back tomorrow afternoon and we'll start learning some competition moves. Turn in your sword if you don't plan to come back. You can hang on to your sword if you want to practice at home. Hope to see you tomorrow!" Johnny dismissed them.

Some students were obviously not coming back. They turned in their swords and went out grumbling and rubbing their arms. Christopher decided to keep his sword. He glanced over at Crystal. She hung back and was the last one in line. Was she going to quit and hand in her sword?

Johnny smiled at her. "You are a natural, Crystal. I hope you'll be back tomorrow."

Crystal beamed at him and sighed on the inside. He was so handsome. And not that much older than her, really. Just a few years. She wondered...

"Hey Crystal, I was going to call you later to check up on you." Christopher interrupted her thoughts.

"Check...um...huh?" She stumbled over her words, still under Johnny's spell.

"Yeah. Billy kinda threatened you in class today so I thought... never mind." Christopher could see she wasn't really paying attention. To him, that is. He felt a wisp of jealousy start to wrap itself around his heart along with... was that anger? Yep, definitely anger at Johnny.

"I should get home," Christopher told Johnny. "Can you give me a lift?"

"Sure thing buddy," said Johnny. "See you tomorrow, Crystal?"

"Yes. See you tomorrow." Crystal replied dreamily, putting her sword in her backpack like she had seen the other returning students do. She would definitely practice. She wanted to impress Johnny.

At the car, Christopher got in and slammed the door. He said nothing for a few miles. Johnny just whistled the whole way, which made Christopher angrier and angrier.

"What the heck was that?" Christopher finally exploded. "You know I like her, but you made your moves on her anyway."

"Moves? Really, Christopher? I didn't do anything inappropriate. What do you think I did?" The whistling changed to a bouncy little tune Christopher had not heard before and it made him crazy.

"You, you….you smiled at her," he stammered.

"I…smiled?" Johnny raised an eyebrow. He was enjoying this. "You are angry at me because I smiled? I smile at you all the time."

"This is different! You hypnotized her or something!"

"By smiling? Really, Christopher?"

Christopher was silent. "I guess that sounds ridiculous, doesn't it?" he said after a few moments.

"Yes, buddy. Ridiculous." Johnny smiled at Christopher. "But I understand. You really like this girl and she was giving me the attention you wanted, right?"

"Right!" Christopher was surprised that Johnny understood. "How do I get her to notice me?" Christopher's voice began to sound a little whiny. Johnny loved this. Jealousy, anger, whining, and even a little self-pity in there—perfectly in line with his plan.

"Just be yourself. Who could resist you?" Johnny reached over and tousled Christopher's hair. Christopher pushed Johnny's hand away.

"Exactly," Christopher said. "Who could resist me? Zit-face and all." Pouting, he said nothing more all the way home.

CHAPTER 9

Wood shop and fencing were Christopher's two favorite school activities. He did well in all of his classes, but the satisfaction he got from making things out of wood with his own two hands was amazing. He also loved the feeling of power he got while brandishing his sword at fencing practice. He was perfecting the moves. It felt a bit like dancing, moving back and forth with a partner in choreographed rhythm. Both Michael and Johnny were excellent teachers. They didn't play favorites, treating him just like all the other students they worked with. This was good because Billy was looking for any excuse to give him a punch in the nose, and if he was a teacher's pet, well, that would give him the opening he needed.

Mostly, Christopher avoided Billy. He got to biology class just as the bell rang and slipped out as soon as the teacher dismissed them. The teacher had assigned Christopher the seat closest to the door so that was perfect. Easy in. Easy out. He would never make the mistake of being alone in an empty hallway again either.

Christopher hadn't really had the opportunity to talk to Crystal as much as he would have liked, but at least it seemed as if she and Billy had broken up. Billy now hit on all the girls equally and was getting a reputation among the young females for being a slick talker looking for only one thing. None of the girls would give him the time of day anymore, no matter how hard he tried. They seemed to have found a common source of courage and were sticking together. This made Christopher happy. Billy deserved the cold shoulder treatment. He thought he was so good with the ladies, but they were just ignoring him now, like they didn't even see him. Boy! He bet that really bruised Billy's ego! Christopher almost laughed out loud as he imagined Billy on his knees begging for a sliver of encouragement from even the ugliest girl.

Crystal's seat was directly across the room in English class now, near the windows. Christopher wanted to just look at her the whole class period, but in order to do that he had to look past Billy, who was assigned a seat in the middle of the room—third aisle, second seat. He sat up straight and tried to pay attention to the teacher, but his eyes kept wandering to the windows where Crystal sat chewing on her pencil. He sighed. She was so cute! It was hard to think of anything else.

"Christopher?" The teacher's voice interrupted his thoughts. "Are you with us?" The class laughed, and Billy smirked at him, leaning back in his chair.

"Yes, Ms. Ricker."

"Hmmm," she replied and continued with the lecture.

Christopher kept his eyes down after that. It was easier to control where he looked rather than what he was thinking.

After class Christopher hurried out the door, but this time he wasn't fast enough. He had been preoccupied with thoughts of Crystal. Billy walked behind him, purposefully stepping on Christopher's heels as he walked, trying to trip him. "You're such a loser," Billy taunted him in a voice only Christopher could hear. "You're all mushy over a girl—a whore. Crystal's a whore."

Christopher whirled around, his fists clenched. "Take that back!" he said between gritted teeth.

"Why should I? It's true. Crystal's nothing but a whore and she loves Mr. Johnny, not you, because you're such a wimpy loser."

By this time, a small crowd of students was gathering around them.

"I am the king around here," Billy continued. "You are nothing at all. No one likes you so just go home and cry to your mommy, who, by the way, is a whore too."

That did it! Before Christopher could stop himself, he pulled his practice sword out of the side pocket of his book bag and swung it forward, hitting Billy squarely in the chest. It knocked Billy off balance and he fell backward, landing on his butt.

"You are not as tough as you think you are. You are just a weak, little baby. Waaa Waaa! Go cry to your mommy!" Christopher felt exhilarated as he shouted the words. He really could stand up for himself now. Mentally, he thanked Johnny for that.

The students began laughing. Some had their cell phones out recording the whole exchange. Billy looked up in anger and embarrassment. He got up and pointed a finger at Christopher. "Get lost, loser, before I kill you," he threatened. Billy pushed his way through the crowd and disappeared around the side of the building.

Christopher bowed dramatically to the crowd of students before he turned and casually walked away, his head held high. He still heard the students laughing at Billy in his mind even after they were out of sight. He thought it sounded kind of like happy music in a way. He knew he shouldn't have pushed Billy down, but it felt justified, actually. For once he had stood up for himself instead of just trying to avoid trouble. He suspected his grandfather would have been proud of him. His mom and dad, well, probably not.

The video was posted on YouTube within a few minutes and students all over the campus were talking about how Christopher had bested the school bully with a toy sword. Within seconds, and because of him, Billy had become a laughingstock. Christopher smiled. It felt good. High school might not be so bad now. He was getting high-fives from students and even the senior girls were smiling at him.

Christopher slid into his seat in shop class. He found he wasn't slouching today or trying to avoid everyone. No. In fact, he seemed to be more confident and met the admiring gazes of his classmates without looking away. He grinned.

Michael pulled Christopher aside during the independent work time at the end of the period and spoke quietly to him about the video. "You hurt Billy today," he began.

"No, I didn't," interrupted Christopher. "He was fine. He got right up and threatened to kill me. I think I was justified in what I did. He called Crystal a whore and he called my Mom a whore. He deserved what he got."

"Maybe," said Michael, "But it really wasn't up to you to deal out the punishment. He may not have been hurt physically, but you hurt him in other ways. There will be consequences that you may not have considered."

"Good," said Christopher. "He needed to learn that he can't bully others without consequences. I was happy to give him that lesson and I would do it again. It actually felt good to stand up for myself for a change and not be afraid. I felt like, well, like my grandpa. He's the boss and no one messes with him. I want to be just like that."

Christopher looked down at the phone in his hand. "Wow! The YouTube video already has 149,237 likes!" He read through the comments people had posted. "Loser!" "What a geek!" "Go kill yourself, wimp!" "Beaten by a toy! What a joke!"

"Christopher D'Antoni, please report to the principal's office immediately." A nasally female voice echoed through the classroom PA system. "Christopher D'Antoni, report to the principal's office."

Christopher grinned. No more wimpy nice guy. This was actually fun. He spun on his heels and left the room without noticing the disappointed look on Michael's face.

"Mr. D'Antoni, come in." The principal's secretary was a plump, 60-something year old matron with gray hair pulled back into a bun. She tried to look professional, but her too-tight blazer and too-loose skirt just looked ridiculous to him. She was nice, though, and always had hard candy on her desk for anyone coming in for any reason—good or bad. Christopher helped himself and sat down to wait in the most comfortable of the three office chairs along the wall. It wasn't long before the principal opened his door and waved Christopher inside. He slowly walked to his desk and sat down.

"Hey, Mr. Castillo, what's up?" Christopher was still grinning. He couldn't seem to help it. He took the seat opposite the principal and leaned back in the chair.

"Well, Christopher, I don't know quite how to begin." He cleared his throat. "It seems that you and Billy had a bit of a fight today."

"It wasn't much of a fight, Mr. Castillo," Christopher interjected. "He has bullied me since the first day of school. He just got what was coming to him, that's all."

"You hit him with a sword."

"It was a practice sword—a wooden sword that didn't hurt him at all. It just surprised him and knocked him down.

He was fine. He got right up and threatened to kill me. Yeah, that's right," Christopher continued. "He threatened to kill me so I think you had better call him in here and punish him, not me. I didn't do anything except defend myself."

"I saw the video," Mr. Castillo continued.

"So you know I'm telling the truth."

"Yes. I heard and saw everything on the video. What I haven't seen—or even heard about until now—was that Billy was bullying you."

"He was. You can ask anyone. He needs to be punished."

"I saw the comments people were posting about him. They were very cruel."

"He deserved them, Mr. Castillo. Really, he did."

Mr. Castillo was silent. There was an odd look on his face, like he was trying not to cry. His lips were pushed tightly together and his eyes were squinting and blinking. He turned his head away from Christopher and looked out the window.

"I can't punish Billy," Mr. Castillo said sadly.

"What?! You're taking his side? I've never ever gotten into trouble and you're going to punish me instead of that little dweeb?"

"I can't punish Billy," Mr. Castillo continued, "because he is… he is… no longer with us."

"You expelled him? Excellent!" exclaimed Christopher.

"No. You misunderstand. I can't… he isn't…" Mr. Castillo paused, then continued in one long, slow breath. "Billy is dead, Christopher. He left campus after the YouTube video was posted and people said those things about him. He went home and hung himself in his garage. His mother found him when she came back from the grocery store about a half hour ago. She called 9-1-1 and then me."

There was no sound at all except the tick, tick, tick of the clock on Mr. Castillo's desk. Christopher just stared at Mr. Castillo for about a minute, then said in hushed tones, "Uh. I didn't know."

"Sometimes bullies are bullies for a reason," Mr. Castillo said. "They are usually the opposite of who they try to project they are. Billy had problems. We were trying to help him, but…unfortunately, we failed."

Christopher had no reply so Mr. Castillo continued, "The cruel words posted were just too much for him. They confirmed everything he really thought about himself and he decided to just end his own life."

"I didn't post anything," Christopher defended himself. "It wasn't my fault."

"No, Christopher, it wasn't your fault. I just thought you should know before it gets out. It will most likely be on the news, and the press may want to talk to you since you were the other person in the video."

Christopher almost said, "Cool!" but caught himself before the words left his mouth. He was sorry about Billy but couldn't help feeling a bit excited at the thought of being a celebrity.

"Thanks for telling me, Mr. Castillo." Christopher got up from his chair and headed toward the door. "I've got to go to fencing practice now, if that's OK?"

Mr. Castillo just nodded and swung his chair around toward the window so his back was to Christopher. He gave a weak little wave over his head as Christopher opened the door and left.

The atmosphere was subdued as Christopher walked into the gym for fencing practice. The word was out. Billy was dead and, at least for this moment in time, some students were sad about it. He didn't think they were sad about Billy in particular. He thought they were just sad or feeling guilty that someone died and their posts might have contributed to that. The looks they were giving him weren't admiration. They were...well, maybe shared guilt? But he didn't feel guilty. Should he feel guilty?

"Hi Christopher." Johnny came over and put his hand on Christopher's shoulder. "How are you doing?"

"I'm fine. Why?"

"I thought you might be upset about Billy."

"Well, geez, he must have been mental to have killed himself over a few comments on YouTube. He didn't die because of me. Why should I be upset? I didn't like him. He bullied me. Everyone knows that. There was something seriously wrong with him."

The other fencing students gathered around Christopher and Johnny.

"No worries," Tony assured him. "We all know Billy was a jerk. Did you get in trouble with the principal? Is that why he called you to the office today?"

"I am NOT in trouble! Why should I be in trouble? The principal just wanted to tell me, that's all, in case the press comes around to talk to me."

"The press? Wow. That's cool," said Crystal. The other students agreed and that look of admiration crept back onto their faces as they looked at Christopher.

"Let's get ready for practice." Johnny shooed the students off to the locker rooms to change.

Christopher was in no hurry. He knew he had been a bit defensive because he was feeling just a little guilty about Billy. Johnny put an arm around Christopher's shoulders as they walked toward the boys' locker room and said, "What Billy did is not your fault, and things happen for a reason, so there is no need for you to feel guilty about any of it, OK?"

"OK. Thanks, Johnny."

"OK. Now suit up." Johnny grinned and slapped Christopher playfully on the back. "You showed great form on the YouTube video. I was proud of you for that. Keep that up and you might be fencing champion this year!"

"Thanks!" Christopher returned Johnny's grin with one of his own and hurried off to change.

CHAPTER 10

The press was outside his house. Christopher could see them from a block away as he walked home from practice. Yikes! He wanted to tell them his side of the story, but he was nervous. He liked being the center of attention in his family, but this was city-wide center of attention—heck, maybe even country-wide center of attention! He hung back for just a moment before continuing his walk home.

One of the reporters saw him and came running, microphone in hand. The others followed, all with microphones and cameramen. He heard the first reporter say, "We are live in front of the home of Christopher D'Antoni, the student who is at the center of this controversy." She waved the camera man forward and thrust the microphone toward Christopher.

"What can you tell us about Billy Jones? Is it true Billy is dead because of the fight between the two of you today?"

"What?" Christopher was stunned. Were they blaming him? "No. No, that's not it at all."

"But you did fight him today in school?"

"It wasn't really a fight. He said my friend was a whore and my mother was a whore so I just knocked him down with my practice sword. He wasn't even hurt."

"Here is a clip of the video," the reporter said to the camera. She waited a few minutes while someone somewhere played the YouTube video for everyone watching live on TV. Christopher fidgeted uneasily.

"We're back live with Christopher D'Antoni. Christopher, tell us what you know about Billy's death."

"Well, Mr. Castillo told me he hung himself in his garage."

"Mr. Castillo?"

"Yes, that's my principal. He said Billy was upset about the comments made and went home and hung himself. He must have been mental to do something like that, right?"

"Do you think embarrassing him by knocking him down with your sword had anything to do with his mental state when he killed himself?"

"No way! It was not my fault. Everyone says so."

"Everyone?"

"My principal, my teachers, even the rest of the students say it was not my fault. Billy was a bully. He bullied me. He bullied Crystal. He bullied others too. Someone had to stand up to him."

"So you see yourself as the hero of this story?" asked the reporter.

"Yes," said Christopher firmly. "I defended myself and others from Billy. What he did afterward was his own choice. It was not my fault he took it to the extreme. He could have just apologized and changed his ways and things would have been different for him. He didn't have to go hang himself. That was crazy."

"Were you behind any of the comments posted on YouTube?"

"I didn't post anything. I don't know who did."

"Do you think people should have said those things about Billy?"

"Everyone has free speech rights, don't they? They are entitled to their own opinions. It just shows you Billy didn't make too many friends by bullying all of us. If he had been a better person, no one could have or would have said those things, right?" Christopher was getting angry now. She should just stop trying to make him feel responsible for Billy's stupid decision.

The reporter backed off a little. Another reporter stepped up and asked, "Would you do anything differently if you could start this day over?"

Christopher just looked at him and blinked. He had had enough. He pushed his way through and walked the remaining 100 feet home with the reporters following and shouting questions. He ran up the steps, opened the front door, went in, and shut the door firmly behind him. Maybe this celebrity thing wasn't so great after all.

He peeked out the window to see if they were gone. Nope. Still there. What were they waiting for? Oh shit! His mother drove into the driveway next to the house and got out of the car. She opened the trunk and took out the bag of groceries that would undoubtedly be tonight's dinner. Christopher saw her turn around. He saw her look of surprise as the reporters blocked her entry to the house, asking questions all at the same time. The cacophony of voices was unsettling. He could hear them through the window but couldn't make out what they were asking. He saw his mom drop the grocery bag and put one hand over her mouth and the other over her heart. She looked horrified. She pushed her way through the reporters without saying a word and ran into the house. She locked the door behind her and stood there staring at Christopher.

"They said…they are saying…they claim…that a boy is dead because of you," she stammered in a whisper.

"That's a lie!" Christopher protested. "I didn't even know him. He was just a kid in school that kept threatening me and calling you a…" Christopher paused before continuing. "A… bad name," he finished weakly.

Teresa took Christopher's hand in hers and led him into the kitchen away from the front windows. They sat quietly at the table for a long minute before she asked, "What happened?"

"It wasn't my fault," Christopher said flatly.

"What wasn't your fault?"

"That Billy hung himself."

Teresa held back a gasp. Instead, she took a deep breath and said calmly, "Tell me what happened."

"Billy has been on my case since the beginning of school this year. I tried to avoid him, Mom, really I did, but he just kept coming at me. His girlfriend broke up with him and people started to realize what a jerk he is, er, was. Today he called Crystal a whore and you a…the same thing…and I just lost it. I knocked him down with my practice sword and everyone laughed at him. Someone posted it on YouTube and people started commenting. Mr. Castillo said Billy had mental problems and that just pushed him over the edge. He went home and hung himself in his garage."

Teresa was silent, but her eyes filled with tears. "Oh my god, how awful," she said.

"Yeah," Christopher replied.

"Did you…did you post anything…on the YouTube video, I mean?" she asked.

"Nah. I wouldn't do that, Mom."

"Good," she said. "Good."

There was a knock at the back door. It opened slightly and Johnny peeked in through the crack. "OK if I come in?" He was holding the bag of groceries Teresa had dropped.

"Of course, Johnny," Teresa said shakily. "You are always welcome. Did you hear about what happened today? How did you get past the reporters?"

"Oh, I sent them away," Johnny said nonchalantly, setting the groceries on the counter. "They have no business harassing you."

"Thank you! I don't know how you did it, but thank you! Joseph will be home soon and he would have been so angry. They accused Christopher of killing that poor boy!"

"That's ridiculous," said Johnny smiling. "You know our boy here wouldn't hurt a fly." He ruffled Christopher's hair playfully.

"But he knocked him down..." Teresa wasn't sure yet how innocent Christopher was but it seemed obvious to Johnny that she was asking for reassurance.

"Self-defense," Johnny interrupted. "And it had nothing to do with why the boy killed himself. A normal kid would have just gotten up and maybe thrown a punch or two and then gone about his business. Billy wasn't normal. His mental problems were there for years. His parents should have known that and taken care of it. Heck! The school should have flagged him and sent him for help or something. His death should be on their consciences, not Christopher's."

Teresa nodded. It made sense. Another knock at the door interrupted the conversation.

"Hi! Everyone OK?" Michael came into the room.

"Yes, everyone is fine." Johnny couldn't help the scowl that crossed his face when Michael came in but he quickly covered it with another of his charming smiles before Christopher or Teresa noticed it.

"I wanted to check in on you, kid, just to be sure."

"I'm OK. Why wouldn't I be?" Christopher replied. "Did you know this would happen? What did you mean today when you said there might be consequences for what I did?"

Now Johnny couldn't help but smile. Michael was being challenged. Maybe this would turn around to be his fault. If he could just steer the conversation a bit in that direction...

Michael sighed and began to explain. "Sometimes when we act in anger or without thinking, things happen as a result that are not always what we expect. For example, you probably thought that Billy would learn his lesson after you knocked him down and not bother you anymore and that would be it, right?"

"Yeah, and that he would know what it felt like to not be so popular, like me."

"So, for you, the consequence that you visualized was that he would stop bothering you and life would be good for both of you from that point on?"

"Yeah, sure, OK," Billy said.

"Or did you just want revenge, regardless of the consequences?"

"I guess I wasn't thinking about consequences. Just about getting him to stop bullying me."

"That's what I meant. When we don't think about consequences, sometimes what happens is not what we expect or want."

"Are you saying Billy's death is Christopher's fault?" Johnny interrupted with feigned surprise.

"Oh, Michael, you don't believe that, do you?" Tears began rolling down Teresa's face. "I can't believe you would blame him! Stop! Just stop!" She put her hands over her ears and ran from the room.

"You twisted my words, Johnny," Michael said slowly. "Again."

"Everyone heard you say them, Michael," Johnny said sarcastically. "Don't pay any attention to him, Christopher. It was not your fault at all."

"But..." Christopher mumbled. "But maybe I should have...I was really angry...I wanted him gone..."

"Of course you felt that way," Johnny comforted him. "Feelings like that come and go. You didn't act on your feelings. You didn't kill him. He killed himself. That was not your fault."

Michael looked sadly at them both. "If you want to talk more about it, Christopher, I would gladly listen."

"No he doesn't, do you buddy?" Johnny said, putting an arm protectively around Christopher's shoulders. "He's fine."

Christopher just shrugged.

Teresa came back into the room, wiping her eyes. "I've got to get dinner ready. Joseph will be home soon. Do you boys want to stay for dinner tonight?"

"Sure," said Johnny.

"Yes," said Michael.

Christopher sighed with relief. Teresa gave him a hug and then shooed the three of them out the back door. "Go on, then, and shoot some hoops or something while I cook."

Christopher had to give the full story again when his father came home that night. He inserted a few more details to make it exciting. Exaggerated a bit maybe, but not so much that it was actually lying. When he got to the part where he knocked Billy down with his sword, he was pretty sure he saw a glimmer of pride in his father's eyes. Johnny gave him a high-five and told his dad that he had award-winning form as a fencer. Teresa looked away, and Michael looked angry. He had never seen Michael angry before. That was interesting.

His father listened intently to the rest of the story and swore when Christopher told him about how Billy had hung himself. "That kid was really messed up, huh?" Joseph said when Christopher finished.

"Yeah, he was really messed up," Christopher agreed.

"So why are people saying it was your fault? I'm not sure I understand that part." Joseph looked puzzled. "There doesn't seem to be any connection to you at all. You didn't film it. You didn't post it or repost it. You didn't comment."

"Exactly!" said Johnny.

"But it wouldn't have happened if…" Michael tried to interject.

"You don't know that. The kid was mental," Johnny said firmly.

"Well, we won't argue about it. We support you, Christopher," said Joseph. "And those reporters and idiots can just go find someone else to blame."

"Thanks, Dad," said Christopher. He smiled at all of them and they all smiled at him in return. All except Michael, that is. Michael still looked angry and sort of sad. Hmmm. He wondered what that was all about.

CHAPTER 11

I t took about two weeks before the students forgot about Billy, before the news reporters gave up and moved on to other stories, and before Christopher could relax and put the whole mess behind him. Yesterday, Saturday, his mom had made him go to confession just in case he had even a small part in the...event...but he had told the priest all of Billy's faults and none of his own. The priest had absolved him, so he shoved the guilt aside and locked it in a hidden compartment of his mind.

Life was actually good. Crystal wasn't afraid to hang out with him now. Sometimes he still caught her gazing adoringly at Johnny but since he didn't respond or encourage her, Christopher was OK with that. He adored Johnny too. Not in a weird way, though, just in a mentor and best friend kind of way. Christopher was now one of the popular kids in school and he credited Johnny for helping make that happen. Everyone thought Johnny was cool, and he was Johnny's friend, so they thought he was cool too. Being handsome helped too. The girls were noticing him and he could have his pick if he wanted it. He still liked Crystal but found his thoughts were not always about her anymore. He fantasized about other girls, too.

It was Sunday morning and Christopher was allowed to sleep in if he wanted to so he was in no hurry to get out of bed. His mom would be going to church. His dad would be outside polishing his new car. They went to Nonno's and Momma's house each week for Sunday dinner but that was hours from now. He had nothing to do at the moment to relieve his boredom except think about girls. Christopher put his hands behind his head and gazed at the ceiling. He was startled from his reverie by the sound of his cell phone ringing. He reached over and grabbed it.

"Hello," Christopher said sleepily.

"Hi Christopher!" It was Michael. "I thought this might be a good day to go fishing if you're up for it."

"Fishing? Really? I've always wanted to go fishing."

"Can you be ready in half an hour?"

"Yeah! Sure! Cool!"

Michael laughed. "I'll see you soon then."

Michael arrived exactly 30 minutes later. Christopher had been ready and waiting for at least 20 minutes. He was embarrassingly excited, he thought, although when he told his mom where he was going he sounded very nonchalant in his own mind. He took a deep, calming breath before dashing out the front door. He hugged his dad goodbye. Geez! He hadn't done that in years. He grinned and climbed into Michael's Jeep.

"Let's go!"

Michael grinned back and put the Jeep into first gear. "Let's go!"

They headed off down the road toward Wampus Pond in Armonk.

"I got fishing licenses for us." Michael tossed them to Christopher. "And I reserved a rowboat."

Christopher laughed. "A rowboat? I was imagining something a little less work."

"Nah. It'll be fun," Michael said, still grinning. "We'll row out to a quiet spot and put out our fishing poles."

"I suppose you're renting those too?" Christopher asked.

"No. I bought them. They're in the back."

"Cool," said Christopher. "Bait? Did you bring bait?"

"Yes I did. Nice juicy worms behind your seat in the cooler."

"Oh!" Christopher picked up his feet and put them on the dashboard. "You thought of everything. How did you pull this together so fast?"

"Been thinking about it and planning it for a couple of weeks, ever since…you know. I thought it would be good to just get away for a bit."

"Oh," Christopher said. "Johnny didn't want to come?"

"I didn't ask him to. I thought it would be nice to have you all to myself," Michael teased.

Christopher was silent. It was nice. Being with Johnny was fun and exciting and always a bit daring. Being with Michael was peaceful and calming. He needed a break from the adrenaline rush he always got from being with Johnny. Michael was right. He needed this.

Michael pulled into a parking spot close to the boat rental office. The boat was ready and waiting for them. They took the rods and the bait from the Jeep and headed down to the lake.

Christopher had never rowed before but he caught on quickly. They took turns until they found a quiet, secluded spot near the northern end of the lake. Michael was a patient teacher. He showed Christopher how to cast, then how to bait the hook. Christopher's first real cast was a good one. They sat in comfortable silence for a while, listening to the sounds of the birds and the frogs near the shore.

"Hey! I see a turtle. Look! There! There!" Christopher was excited. He pointed to a head just breaking the surface about ten feet away.

"Cool!" Michael said. "Looks like a young snapping turtle."

A hawk circled overhead. "Should we help him or something? That hawk looks hungry." Christopher was worried.

Michael smiled. "No. He has to make his own way. If we pick him up he could get turned around and never find his way home again."

"But the hawk…"

"Turtles have hard shells to protect them. That hawk will never be able to get his talons into him as long as the turtle uses the protection God gave him. If he leaves his neck out or his feet out, well, that's a different story. Foolish, too, since he has an easy escape from the danger just by pulling his head and legs into the shell."

"Can he do that while swimming, though? Isn't he exposed in the water?"

"He can stay submerged for about a half an hour. Long enough for the hawk to get discouraged and go elsewhere for his snack."

"That is super cool!" Christopher exclaimed.

"Yes, it is," replied Michael. "Kind of like humans in a way. They have all the protection they need. Some use it. Some don't."

"Protection against what?"

"Against the evil in the world that tries to entice you by pretending it is good or at least by making excuses for why it isn't bad."

Christopher thought about that. "How can evil pretend it is good? That doesn't make sense. Everyone knows what evil is. Murder, for example. Murder is evil. No one can pretend murder is good."

Michael shook his head slowly. "Oh, but they do. Abortion, for example. That is murdering unborn children, yet this society believes it is good. In ancient times, people used to sacrifice their children after they were born—kill them and burn them—and say it was good. From then until now humans have not always recognized evil for what it is until it is too late—until the hawk has them in its claws and is about to devour them. Very few people would intentionally choose evil, yet they do choose it because they have been deceived into thinking it is good, or justified in some way."

Christopher thought for a minute. "Well, I'm not going to murder anyone."

"There are other types of evil, Christopher, that are more subtle yet just as destructive," Michael replied. "Lying, hate, envy, cheating, pride…"

"I wouldn't classify those as evil," Christopher protested. "Character flaws, maybe, but evil—no. Evil is the really bad stuff, I think. Doing evil things is what gets you sent to Hell. I only had to say ten Hail Marys for cheating on my math test, so I'm not going to Hell for that."

The water gently lapped against the side of the boat but there was no other sound. It was like nature was holding her breath, waiting. But waiting for what?

"Nobody goes to Hell for being evil or doing wrong," Michael said firmly.

"What? That's not what the priest says. You should go to church, Michael. They teach you that stuff there."

"They go to Hell for rejecting the Savior."

"You mean Jesus? The guy that is hanging on the cross? My mom has a few of those around the house."

"Yes, Jesus. He's like the turtle shell that protects you when evil tries to catch you. But unless you decide to pull in your head and feet, He can't do anything to save you. It's your choice. You can accept and use the shell or reject the shell."

"That's just weird."

Michael laughed. "I know. It's not a perfect analogy. But do you understand the message I'm trying to give you?"

"Not really," said Christopher. "Hey, I think I got a fish!" He pulled at the line and saw the fish tail flapping in the water.

"Reel him in!" cried Michael. "Your first fish! Wow! It's a big one!"

Together they reeled in the fish and put him in the cooler. Christopher was smiling from ear to ear. "Take my picture with it, please?" he begged.

"Sure!" Michael took several pictures with Christopher's cell phone.

"I can't wait to send these to Johnny!" Christopher exclaimed. "He'll flip out!"

"OK," said Michael, looking at his watch. "Time to go home."

"Thanks for bringing me, Michael. Maybe we can do this again sometime?"

"Absolutely," said Michael. "That would be great!"

Michael rowed back to the dock, mentally talking to his father. "What do I do now?" There was no answer, of course. It was all in his head.

Christopher chattered all the way home about the turtle, about catching the fish, about his friends, about girls, about his summer plans—about everything but what Michael thought was really important. Time was running out.

CHAPTER 12

His sophomore year of high school would definitely be better than his freshman year. Christopher was sure of it. He was already popular, and he knew he would do well in his classes. He had almost won the state fencing championship last year, which only added to his popularity. Driving up to the front of the school with Johnny on the first day of tenth grade was not even close to a deja vu. There was nothing similar about this first day of school except the yellow Corvette he was riding in. The admiring looks were for him as well as for Johnny this time. The girls blew him kisses, the boys waved. He was on top of the world.

The summer had flown by. He dated Crystal—and Jane, and Kelly, and Alyssa, and Jennifer, and Nicole, and a few others. None of them exclusively. They all knew that and accepted it, except maybe Crystal. She had said no the last time he asked her to go to the movies. She was still nice to him, though, so it wasn't like she was mad or anything. He shrugged. He wasn't sure why he had been so head over heels about her last year. She wasn't the prettiest girl or the smartest girl in the school. Lately she had just seemed sad—a real drag sometimes. So Christopher wasn't all that upset that she had turned him down. He preferred happy girls that were excited to be with him.

As he got out of the car, a girl with blonde hair and a summer tan ran over and linked her arm in his. "Hey handsome! I missed you!"

"I missed you too," said Christopher, trying to remember her name. "How was your summer, uh, Lizzie?"

She gave him a sideways glance and giggled. "Silly! I was in Idaho with my grandparents. How do you think it was? Ugggh!" She gave a pretend shiver. "I am so glad to be back, aren't you?"

"Sure am!"

"Hey, I tried this new...thing...while I was in Idaho. You'll love it! I brought some back for you." Lizzie let go of his arm and held out two beige tablets. On one side was stamped AD, on the other was a 30.

"Where did you get those?" Christopher asked. "What is it?"

"I got them from my brother. He was diagnosed with ADHD and the doctor prescribed Adderall. He refused to take them, so I helped myself. I tried it and, wow, I have so much more energy now. The world is great. Isn't it great, Christopher?" Lizzie reached out and took Christopher's hand in both of hers, slipping the pills into his palm. "Just try it. It can't hurt you. It just gives you a bit more energy to get through the day. You'll feel great, I promise."

Christopher put the pills in his jacket pocket. "Thanks Lizzie. Maybe later. I've got to get to class now. See you!" He hurried up the front steps and into the building. Just before he went inside, he glanced over his shoulder and saw Lizzie talking to another boy—Sean, he thought—and Johnny still sitting in the Corvette watching him with a smile.

Why did that bother him, he wondered? Lizzie was a flirt, so that was not unusual. But Johnny must have heard the conversation—they had been standing just outside the car—and he was smiling? He would have to ask him about that later. Now, he had woodworking class.

Michael and Johnny must have done well last year because the principal had asked them back again. Michael was not just a guest lecturer this year. He was the actual teacher. That was really cool. Christopher knew this was a class he would definitely get an A in and not just because Michael liked him. He worked hard because he really liked it. He was considering becoming a carpenter like Michael. People made good money in the trades. His dad wanted him to be a lawyer, but Christopher thought a trade like carpentry might suit him better. Oh well, lots of time to figure that out.

"Welcome back everyone!" Michael was genuinely happy to see the students. "This is your second year of woodworking so we're going to be doing more complicated projects. You'll design your own instead of using pre-made plans, so I am looking forward to seeing your creativity unleashed."

The first year had weeded out the students who were just trying to earn an easy credit. All eleven of the students in this year's class were here because they really liked it. Make that twelve students. Tony dashed through the door just as the bell rang.

"Sorry Mr. Michael. I just got my schedule fixed." Tony handed Michael a pass from the guidance department.

"Glad you made it, Tony. Why don't you sit with Christopher. The two of you can be partners for the first project."

Christopher gave Michael an incredulous look. "Me? I was going to partner with…"

"Thanks, Christopher," Michael interrupted. "The first assignment is to create a chair. It can rock or stand still. It can be any height and width. There are no rules except to use your imagination to figure out a design for a chair that is unique, comfortable, sturdy, and useful. You will be working in pairs. I want to see good teamwork here. Take out a piece of paper and a pencil, and let's get to work!"

The class quickly divided into pairs and began talking about their ideas. Christopher slumped in his chair, sulking. He had wanted to partner with, well, anyone else. Tony annoyed him. He still had the braces and talked with a nasal twang in his voice. The acne was clearing up, but his clothes—wow. They looked as if he had raided the reject bins at the Salvation Army. Nothing matched, and they were usually way too big. He had a habit of hitching up his pants every few minutes that was super weird.

"Hi, Christopher. How was your summer?" Tony asked.

"Fine." Christopher's terse answer, grumpy tone, and crossed arms did not invite conversation, but Tony totally missed the clues.

"Mine too," said Tony cheerfully. "I got a job mowing lawns, so that kept me pretty busy. One of the customers was Billy's mom. She is really nice. She gave me lemonade on the really hot days. Once she baked cookies. Chocolate chip. Man, were they good!"

"Blah, blah, blah," was what Christopher heard. He really didn't care about Tony's summer. He didn't really care about Tony.

"And another one of the customers was Crystal's family. She has a really nice house. Not like Billy's mom. Her house is kinda like mine—kinda run-down, ya know? Anyway, Crystal's house is like a mansion or something. It took me two hours to do that lawn. And she has a swimming pool in her backyard. How cool is that? She was usually swimming or sitting by the pool getting a tan in a bikini—a bikini, dude! I sure didn't mind working there, that's for sure. She is hot!" Tony shook his fingers as if they were on fire.

Christopher scowled. He definitely did not like the idea of Tony looking at Crystal's body or commenting on it like that. It was OK for him to look, but not Tony. That was gross. Tony was gross. He was sure Crystal would think that too.

"And she is very nice," Tony continued. "After I finished the lawn, we would sit and talk about stuff. Hey, you guys aren't still going out are you? I was thinking I might ask her."

Christopher looked at Tony in surprise. "She won't go out with you," he blurted without thinking.

Tony shrugged. "Maybe not. But she's nicer than the other girls. She just might feel sorry for me and say yes," he joked. "But really, Christopher, I think she likes me, at least a little. I don't know much about girls but I'm thinking why else would she stay and talk to me every week? She could hide out in her house, but she doesn't. She comes out when I go over to mow and then offers me a drink and stays and talks. I think I'm falling for her, dude. That is, if you don't like her anymore. I would never make a move on your ladies, Christopher. Honest, I wouldn't. You say the word and I'm done."

Christopher just stared at him. Tony with Crystal? Impossible. But it might be entertaining to watch him bumble his way through this. "Go for it Tony. She's all yours."

"Hey, man. Thanks." Tony grinned, showing his braces. "I will. I'll ask her out today." He hummed happily under his breath—another annoying habit, Christopher noticed. How was he ever going to concentrate on this project?

Christopher chewed on his pencil, trying to think about chairs and chair designs. He drew a rectangular box. Good start, he thought sarcastically. He had a seat. Nothing else. Just a seat. A rectangular, boring seat.

Tony's head was bent over his paper and he was sketching earnestly. Christopher tried to peek, but Tony's arm was wrapped around the left edges of the paper, blocking his view.

"Whatcha got?" Christopher asked him. Tony pushed the paper over so Christopher could see it. He had drawn a straight back chair with the back made out of the letters C-R-Y-S-T-A in 3D and the seat in the shape of an L.

Christopher rolled his eyes and shoved the paper back toward Tony. "Nope. Not doing that," he said.

"How are you boys doing?" Michael asked, coming over to their table. He saw Tony's design.

"That's interesting and unique," he told them, smiling. "But it doesn't look very comfortable. Keep brainstorming."

Christopher was embarrassed. "I haven't come up with anything yet. That's Tony's design. He thinks Crystal likes him."

"Oh, I see. She's a nice girl. Good choice, Tony."

"Thanks, Mr. Michael. I'm going to ask her out today," Tony said in a conspiratorial whisper. "I've been praying she'll say yes."

"Praying?" Christopher asked skeptically. "Don't you mean hoping? Praying? For real?"

"Yeah, for real," Tony said. "I pray now and then. When it's important."

Michael looked thoughtful. "Praying is good, Christopher. In fact, praying is important. We can't … I mean, it is difficult for things to happen or change without prayer. Praying can be very powerful."

Christopher wrinkled his face in disbelief. "Yeah, right. Magic. Poof." He closed and opened both hands in a quick motion, mocking them. "Say the words and all your dreams come true."

"No," replied Michael. "Your dreams may not come true. Praying is not making genie wishes, Christopher. Praying is talking with God. You can ask Him for things, sure, but He may say no if it is in your best interest. Just like your parents sometimes tell you no when you want something that isn't good for you—like having four helpings of ice cream. It may seem good at the time, but you are sorry later when you get a stomachache."

"Hey, that's good, Mr. Michael." Tony beamed. "I never thought of just talking to God. The priest says we should talk to him instead and not bother God so much. Do you think God would really listen to me? I mean, I'm not all that good and I haven't gone to confession in years. The priest says God is holy and can't stand sin or sinners. That's why we have to go through the priest so he can absolve us from our sins and then he can talk to God for us."

"God says he wants everyone to come to Him," Michael answered. "He made a way for you to do that directly."

"Really? How come Father Giovanni never told us that?" Tony was curious. Christopher just fidgeted and continued to chew on his pencil, eyes cast down toward his paper as if he was working on the assignment.

Michael glanced at Christopher, then continued to answer Tony. "Really. Have you ever read the Bible, Tony?" he asked. "It's all in there. God actually came to earth in human form."

"Yeah! I know that story!" Tony said excitedly. "Baby Jesus, right? And he grew up and was a good man. He helped a lot of people and then was killed. He had twelve friends that kept the stories going and started the church."

"Ah, well, that's a broad outline of what happened," said Michael. "His name is Jesus. He did help a lot of people by healing them. And He was killed. But, here's the thing—He didn't stay dead. For three days He fought Satan, conquered death, and won back the earth and the people of the earth. After that, He came back to life, left the tomb they put Him in and gave his friends instructions to tell everyone how to be saved from death too. He took all of the people who had already died and believed in Him back to Heaven with Him. Those that were still alive would need to make a choice. He had won back the right for them to be with Him in Heaven and live forever there with Him, but since humans have free will, they would need to choose that."

Tony was trying to process what Michael had said. He wasn't sure he understood, but it sure sounded good. Christopher rolled his eyes.

"How's this?" Christopher showed Tony and Michael the drawing he had been working on while they had talked. It looked like a throne, with four solid legs, ornately carved arms, a cushioned seat, and a high arched back.

"Nice drawing, Christopher," said Michael. "We can talk later, Tony, if you are interested."

"Sure thing, Mr. Michael. Thanks," said Tony.

Michael put his hand on Christopher's shoulder as if he was going to say something, then shook his head and walked away.

"You don't really believe all that crap, do you?" Christopher asked Tony.

Tony shrugged. "I dunno. I would like to believe that I was that important to somebody," he said.

Chis laughed. "You sure set your sights high. Important to a god? Keep dreaming, man. Even if there was a God, He wouldn't be thinking about you or me. We would be just peons to the gods, Tony. It was a nice story, though," he finished, seeing the look of disappointment on Tony's face. "Wish it were true."

"Yeah, man, whatever," mumbled Tony.

The bell rang. Tony grabbed his book bag and left the room.

"Good luck with Crystal!" Christopher shouted after him, laughing, "And God!"

CHAPTER 13

Christopher ran home after school and threw his jacket over a kitchen chair. Man, was he hungry! School lunches just didn't cut it for curbing hunger—or much of anything else either. The tiny portions they gave them were not even tasty. His only other choice was to make his own lunches in the morning but that was really not an option when he wanted to sleep in to the last second before having to get up and still make it to school on time. It took him 5 minutes, 27 seconds from the minute his eyes opened to when he was dressed, teeth brushed, hair in place, and leaving through the front door. Not bad! If he had to make lunch, he would have to get up at least ten minutes earlier. Nah. Not worth it.

Christopher opened the refrigerator door. Leftover pizza! Jackpot! He grabbed a slice and took a huge bite, not bothering to heat it up. Cold pizza was just fine.

"Hi Christopher! How was school?" His mother came through the front door. She was working again but her boss let her end her day at the same time Christopher's school day ended. Sometimes it was early—like today—but when he had after school activities, she stayed at work until dinner time. They would have pizza or Chinese or take out on those days. Christopher was pretty sure it annoyed his father not to have home cooked meals every day, but he didn't mind. Fast food was perfect for getting the food to his stomach fast.

Teresa laughed when she saw Christopher with the pizza. "Growing boys need their food," she said. "And you have grown this year. I think you'll be as tall as Michael and Johnny before long."

Christopher was average height for an almost-16-year-old so he hoped he would still grow. At 5 feet 9 inches he felt short standing next to the twins. But, since he was taller than the girls at school, it didn't bother him much. He figured he would at least grow another couple of inches. If he hit six feet by graduation that would be just fine. Graduation! He liked that thought. Just over two years to go and he would be free of high school.

Teresa picked up Christopher's jacket from the chair. "This is not the place for your jacket, Christopher! You should hang it up when you come home."

"Sorry, Mom. I'll take care of it." He reached out a hand to take the jacket and caught it by the bottom edge. Two pills fell out of the pocket and rolled on the floor, coming to a stop near his mother's feet.

"What is this?"she asked, picking them up.

Christopher didn't know what to say at first. Then he figured the truth might just work.

"A girl at school I hardly know shoved them into my hand at school this morning. I forgot they were there."

His mother looked puzzled. "But what are they?"

"Adderall, I think."

"But why would she give you Adderall? That's a prescription drug."

"I don't know, Mom. She said they would give me energy."

"Did you take any?" Teresa was worried now.

"No, Ma. I didn't take any. I put them in my pocket and forgot all about them. I wouldn't take drugs."

"Good. Good." Teresa took the pills to the sink and washed them down the drain. "I trust you. Thanks for telling me."

"Sure, Ma."

Johnny came in the kitchen door. "Am I interrupting anything?

"Not at all," said Teresa firmly. "Come on in. I was just about to start dinner. What do you feel like? Steak? Fish? Pasta?"

"Anything at all is good," said Johnny. "Do you feel like a little extra fencing practice before dinner, Christopher? I brought a couple of practice swords."

"Sure. I just have to hang up my jacket first." He walked toward the hallway closet with Johnny following close behind. They went out the front door and around to the backyard. Johnny tossed Christopher one of the swords and got into position. Christopher caught the sword but just held it loosely in his hand, head down.

"Hey, what's the matter?" Johnny asked him, standing up straight and dropping his sword to his side.

"My mom found the pills in my jacket pocket."

"Pills? What pills? How'd they get there?" Johnny asked, grinning.

"I know you saw Lizzie give them to me," said Christopher. "And you had the same look on your face then. Why are you smiling? What is so funny?"

"She found them so you didn't take them, right? So no harm done."

"Of course I didn't take them. Did you think I would? Is that why you were smiling? Did you want me to take them?"

"It was only Adderall," said Johnny. "Adderall is prescribed because it is safe to use. It wouldn't have hurt you. It would just make you more alert. You may need that extra pick-me-up someday. You didn't do anything wrong."

Christopher was angry, but he didn't know why. He threw the sword on the ground. "It was somebody else's prescription, Johnny. Not mine. It might hurt me. I don't think you care. I could die if I take drugs! Health Class 101. Remember?" Christopher stomped up the back stairs toward the sliding glass deck doors.

"Hold on a sec," Johnny was at his side in a flash, holding his arm firmly, preventing him from moving even one step more.

"I do care about you." Johnny changed his expression into one of concern. Time to change tactics. "I know for a fact you would not have died from taking two Adderall pills. If I thought you were in any danger I would have stepped in. All high school kids try drugs of one kind or another.

Adderall is just as good as any and probably safer than most. You've had beer. That's a drug—illegal for you. Did it hurt you? Not at all. It made you feel good and got you accepted by the popular crowd. Remember? I promised you that I would show you how to do grown-up things safely. This is one of those things. Alcohol, recreational drugs—these are things that can be used safely if in moderation. I've got your back, brother!"

"I threw up." Christopher shook free and opened the slider door, still angry. "With the beer, I mean. I threw up." He stepped inside still looking behind him and bumped into Michael.

"Oh, hi Michael," Christopher greeted the other twin in surprise. "I didn't see you there."

"I'm always here when you need me," Michael said, ignoring the hatred and malevolence showing for just a split second in Johnny's expression.

"What makes you think I need you—or anyone? Is this about the pills? How did you know what happened? Did Johnny tell you? Did my mom just call you?" Christopher ranted.

"My father told me you might need me," said Michael smiling.

"Your father? I've never even met him. Why is that, Michael? Why do you hide your father from us? I've always had the impression he was a bit of a deadbeat and that you and Johnny are ashamed of him. How the heck did he know about me anyway?"

"He just has a way of knowing these things. He didn't give me details. Just thought you might need a friend right now."

"Well, he was wrong. I just need to be alone right now. Geez! Everybody is in my business!" Christopher pushed his way past Michael and into the house. He went into his bedroom and slammed the door.

Christopher threw himself on his bed without even kicking off his shoes. There! Take that. This little act of rebellion made him feel slightly better. He sighed and closed his eyes. Just then his cell phone rang.

"Hello?"

"Hi Christopher. It's Crystal." Her voice was quiet and shaky.

"Hi Crystal. What's up?" Christopher didn't really want to talk to her. She had turned him down, after all. Now what? Was she calling to make up with him? Probably.

"Um. I wanted to tell you that Tony..." Her voice drifted off.

"This is about Tony? Did he ask you out? He said he was going to ask you out. I'm sorry, Crystal. I should have told him not to bother you. What a dweeb." For a moment, Christopher felt sorry for her.

"Well, yes, he did ask me out. And he is not a dweeb." Crystal sounded defensive. "He's actually quite nice. I got to know him over the summer."

"Yeah, he told me all about your sexy bikini body." Christopher felt like being mean. "Said you were hot. He was drooling all over himself thinking about you."

Crystal was quiet for a minute, then continued, ignoring his comments. "I was going to say yes, but I wanted to check with you to make sure we were really over first."

"What?!" Christopher was shocked. "Let me get this straight. You want to go out with Tony? Geeky, dweeby, short, pimply-faced, metal-teeth Tony? Are you insane?"

Crystal ignored the insults. "So, to be clear. We are over, right?"

"Heck, yeah. If you prefer Tony over me, you are clearly crazy and I don't do crazy. Have a nice life." Christopher hung up the phone. This day couldn't get any worse.

There was a knock on his bedroom door.

"Christopher?" Oh no. It was his father.

Joseph opened the door. "Christopher, I think we need to talk."

Christopher sighed and kept his eyes closed. His father came over to the bed and sat down.

"Your mom told me about the pills and how you got them. I just wanted to tell you how proud I am that you told the truth and that you didn't take them. But…I need to know…were you planning to take them later? Why did you save them?"

Christopher didn't answer. He just lay there with his eyes shut.

"You know, Christopher, I think many kids your age start to experiment with things—drugs, alcohol, sex…"

Joseph was uncomfortable with the conversation and getting no help from Christopher, who remained silent and still.

"Um… Er… I just want you to know you can talk to me and your mom about anything."

No response.

"It's natural to experiment. We just want you to be safe."

Christopher opened his eyes. "That's what Johnny told me."

Joseph was relieved that Christopher was talking now. "He did? And?"

"And nothing. It was no big deal. I didn't take the pills. Some girl gave them to me and I forgot all about them. Don't you think if I was going to experiment…" He said the word "experiment" with a sarcastic twist in his tone. "…I would have done it already? I have no interest in doing anything unsafe either, even though all of you think I would."

"No! No! We don't think you would do anything unsafe on purpose." Joseph stumbled over his words. "We just think you might not realize…"

Christopher closed his eyes again. "I'm not stupid, Dad. Can I please just be alone?"

"Sure. Sure, son. Whatever you need. Dinner will be ready in a bit. I'll see you then."

Joseph backed out of the room and softly closed the door. He was sure it was just teenage moodiness. Christopher would get over it. He was a good kid. Nothing to worry about.

CHAPTER 14

The yellow Corvette pulled up to the curb just as Christopher was leaving school for the day. "Hey buddy! Hop in!"

Christopher jumped over the door and into the front seat next to Johnny. "Cool! Where are we going?"

"It's a surprise," said Johnny. "But you'll like it!"

Johnny drove fast, tires squealing as they turned left out of the school onto the main street. He always drove fast. Today was no different.

"I thought you might need a pick-me-up, a morale booster, something to make you feel appreciated and special." Johnny grinned.

Christopher stared at him. "You are certainly being weird today," he told Johnny.

"The miracle child who was so special to everyone just got in trouble over nothing. I bet that made you feel just rotten."

"It did. No one understands."

Johnny laughed. "I understand. Believe me."

"My parents used to think I could do no wrong. Now they think I do everything wrong."

"My father is the same way," Johnny said.

"You never talk about your father. Is he… I don't know… abusive or something?"

"I don't like to think about him."

"Well, tell me something. So I know you really do understand." Christopher folded his arms and leaned back in the seat.

Johnny gave a shiver and nodded. "We are not on good terms. There were things he didn't want me to do and I did them anyway. He kicked me out."

"Geez, I'm sorry Johnny."

Johnny shrugged. "It was a long time ago. Anyway, now I have you!" Johnny put a hand over and tousled Christopher's hair, teasing.

Christopher pushed his hand away. "Did Michael get kicked out too?"

"Nah. Michael is one of his favorites. That's why he's not around as much as me. He goes home a lot to earn brownie points with our father."

"What the heck did you do to get kicked out? My dad would never kick me out no matter what I did. He would do everything to protect and defend me."

"I hung out with who he called undesirables and stopped doing everything he told me to do. He is a bit of a dictator in my opinion. I have my own life and I want to live it the way I want to."

"I get that," said Christopher. "I'm kinda feeling the same way. Everyone tries to tell me what to do and what not to do like I'm still a child or something. I can make my own decisions. I'm turning sixteen on Friday for Christ's sake!" The exasperation was clear in his voice.

"You should do whatever makes you happy, Christopher." Johnny sounded sympathetic. "Trust me. Your parents don't always know what is best for you. Only you know that."

"Yeah, you're right. They think they know, but they don't really. How could they? They aren't me."

"Exactly," said Johnny as they pulled into a used car dealership and parked next to the only other car in the middle of the lot. It was a bright apple-red 1969 Mustang.

"Look, Johnny! A Mustang. Right next to us! You don't see those in such good condition around here anymore." Christopher was so excited. This was his favorite car of all time. He opened the car door and got out. Johnny came around to his side of the car and the two of them leaned against the Corvette and stared appreciatively at the Mustang, arms folded as if to remove the temptation to touch it.

"Wow! Oh wow! She's a beauty!" Christopher's eyes shone with envy. "Sure wish she was mine!"

Johnny shook hands with an older man who came out of the building to meet them. "Mr. Fazuti, meet my friend Christopher. I wanted to show him that new car you just got in. The red Mustang."

"No way! This is yours?" exclaimed Christopher. "I love Mustangs, especially the old ones. Where did you find it?"

He pumped Mr. Fazuti's hand up and down and almost forgot to let go. Mr. Fazuti smiled and pulled his hand away.

"I thought you'd like to see it," Johnny said, watching Christopher's reaction. "Glad I was right. Feeling better yet?"

Christopher nodded his head vigorously. He couldn't make any words come out. This was like his own private car show with his favorite car ever.

"Damn thing. A fellow brought in this beautiful red Mustang and asked me to keep it for him for a few weeks," Mr. Fazuti explained, giving Johnny a wink. "Wanna take it for a quick spin? I don't think the owner would mind as long as you're careful." The dealer dangled the keys in front of Christopher.

"Awesome. Just awesome." Christopher found his voice. "Can I really?"

Johnny nodded. "You don't have your driving permit yet, but sure—in the parking lot."

Christopher took the keys from Mr. Fazuti and got in the driver's seat. He put both hands lovingly on the steering wheel before letting go just long enough to put on his seatbelt. Johnny opened the passenger door and sat down, adjusting the seat to accommodate his long legs.

"This is awesome, Johnny. Just awesome! I can't believe I'm driving a Mustang!" Christopher couldn't remember a time when he had been so excited.

"OK. You know what to do?" Johnny asked him, buckling his seatbelt.

"Yeah, sure. I've watched you a thousand times." Christopher turned the key and the car started with a purr. He shifted into first gear and carefully pulled out of the parking space. Johnny let him drive around the building several times before telling him to pull up next to his Corvette. They got out of the car and shook hands with Mr. Fazuti again.

"This was the best day ever. Thanks, Mr. Fazuti." Chris was still running on adrenaline, but he remembered his manners. "And please thank the owner for me. I would like to meet him and talk about Mustangs. I'm sure I could learn a lot from him."

"Sure thing kid," Mr. Fazuti said. "Glad you had fun."

All the way home Christopher dreamt about the red Mustang. Someday he would own a cool car like that! He told Johnny all the facts he knew about Mustangs, not stopping to let Johnny get in a word even after they pulled up to the front of his house and he got out of the car. He was still talking about Mustangs as Johnny pulled away, waving and laughing.

CHAPTER 15

Nonno was getting old. He would not discuss it with anyone but it was evident from the way he shuffled his feet when he walked and in the slight hunch of his shoulders. His voice was not quite as strong as it used to be, but the authority and no-nonsense expectation was still there. He had lost weight and appeared frail, but he carried an elaborately carved cane which he waved around and pointed at people with whom he was displeased. Christopher was sure Nonno would use it as a weapon if he needed to, and that he would win, regardless of his age or physical strength now. He wouldn't be surprised if it had hidden levers that released knives or shot bullets. Nonno was very resourceful.

"Well, Grandson," Nonno said, coming through the front door with Joseph not far behind him. "I am here. I would not miss your sixteenth birthday for anything. I was there at your birth, at your christening, and every milestone. This is a milestone. Sixteen! Impossible for the time to have gone by so quickly. Momma, get me and Joseph some wine to toast this young man!" Nonno shouted in the direction of the kitchen where Teresa and Momma were busy getting the food ready for the party. He sat in one of the wingback chairs near the fireplace to wait.

Momma threw up her hands. "That old man is gettin' on my nerves again." She opened a cupboard door, closed it, then opened another one. "Where are your wine glasses, Teresa? For pity's sake, they should be on these shelves!"

"I washed and dried them for the party today. They are over there—on the table." Teresa pointed to the eat-in kitchen area where a variety of wines, beers, and liquor were arranged behind a variety of wine glasses, beer mugs, and shot glasses on the table. An ice bucket sat on either side of the beverage collection.

Momma was getting old too. Christopher watched her hold the recipe cards only inches from her eyes in order to read them. She was still rather stout—not at all frail like Nonno—but she moved much more slowly than she used to. She forgot things and then got a bit grouchy when people said they had told her that already, didn't she remember? She didn't remember and no, she was sure they had never said a word to her about whatever it was. But then she forgot that too, and would resume her humming, or knitting, or cleaning, or gossiping. She was trying to read the recipe cards because she had forgotten how she used to make lasagna. Christopher had never known her to use a recipe before, but his mom just shrugged and let Momma do whatever she wanted. Teresa put a tray of lasagna in the oven without Momma noticing. Momma still had the mixing bowl in front of her and was trying to grate some cheese. She had forgotten all about the wine.

"Momma! I'm waiting!" Nonno shouted from the living room.

"Waiting? What is he waiting for?" Momma was puzzled.

"Never mind, Momma. I'll take care of it." Teresa picked up a bottle of wine and two glasses and took them to Joseph in the living room.

"Here you go. I don't know why you couldn't get them yourself," Teresa complained. "I am busy getting the food ready. I don't have time to wait on you."

Joseph just looked at her blankly, took the glasses and wine, and walked them back into the kitchen and put them on the table where they had been.

"We'll wait for the guests," he said.

Teresa gave a big, exaggerated sigh and went back to her cooking. Momma had spilled grated cheese everywhere. "Momma, why don't you go sit in the living room with Christopher? I have everything under control here."

"Christopher? Oh, I love Christopher," she said smiling brightly.

Teresa took her by the arm and led her into the living room.

"Christopher, keep an eye on your grandmother, would you?" Teresa said.

"Sure thing, Mom." Christopher didn't mind. Momma could be very entertaining with her stories about the people she knew or thought she knew. He helped Momma into the second wingback chair near the fireplace and then brought over a folding chair so he could sit beside her.

"Tell me about when you turned sixteen, Momma. Did you have a party?"

"Oh, did I!" she exclaimed, launching into a story from her past as other guests began to arrive. It was the same family crowd that came to everything. Aunt Fanny and Uncle Jack, some great aunts and uncles, cousins… yikes, was that Tony? Oh yeah, he did say he was related somehow, or used to be anyway. And Crystal was with him! This was not good.

Christopher gave up his seat to Fanny. His grandmother didn't even pause her story to take a breath as they switched places. One set of ears was just as good as another.

"Thanks, Aunt Fanny." Christopher gave her a quick kiss on the cheek and then slipped away to see who else was arriving.

"No problem, Sweetie," she said, settling in and giving Momma her undivided attention.

A yellow Corvette pulled up in front and slipped expertly into a very tight parking space on the street.

"Johnny!" Christopher waved. "Where's Michael?"

Johnny shrugged. "Dunno. On his way, I guess."

Michael's jeep pulled into the driveway.

"Oh, there he is!" Christopher said. "I'm glad you both could be here!"

"Wouldn't miss it, buddy," said Michael, handing him a wrapped rectangular box about the size of a tablet with a big blue bow.

"Me either," said Johnny, handing Christopher a very small, wrapped box with no bow. "I can't wait for you to see what's inside this! I think you'll love it."

Christopher laughed. "Well, it's pretty small to contain a video game or a computer... Let's see," he said shaking it. "Cufflinks? With my initials? You shouldn't have!"

Johnny laughed. "You'll just have to wait and see!"

The three of them went inside. Christopher put the gifts on the hall table along with the others left there by the arriving guests. They helped themselves to lasagna and salad. Johnny had a beer. Christopher and Michael just had water. The other guests lined up at the buffet table after them and heaped their plates with the food Teresa and Momma had put out.

"Oh no, here comes Crystal. Let's get outa here!" Christopher wanted to avoid her at all costs. He was sort of angry at her for choosing Tony over him. Even though he had told her they were through, he still liked her more than he would admit to anyone.

"Hey Tony!" Michael waved as Tony and Crystal made their way through the crowd of adults. "Hi Crystal. It was nice of you to come celebrate Christopher's birthday."

Michael had spoken up too fast for Johnny to get Christopher away. Johnny scowled at Michael before putting on a smile that seemed almost genuine. "Hi, Tony. Hi, Crystal."

"I hope you don't mind that we came, Christopher." Crystal seemed embarrassed. "But I did want to wish you a happy birthday. You meant—you mean a lot to me even though we broke up, and I hope we can stay friends."

Tony was grinning. "Thanks, man, for setting her free. I'm on top of the world, Christopher, that she could like a guy like me. Amazing, huh?" He put his arm around Crystal's waist and gave it a little squeeze. She smiled up at him.

"A friend like you, the miracle boy, and a girlfriend like Crystal, who is just like an angel. A miracle boy and an angel are my friends. Wow. I am the luckiest guy that ever lived."

Christopher didn't know whether Tony was being serious so he just rolled his eyes and said, "Help yourselves to the food. My mom made it. It's good."

As Tony and Crystal turned around to get in line, Johnny took Christopher's arm

"Would you like to go outside for a while? I brought a cigar for you. You don't inhale so it's perfectly safe. I'll ask your dad to join us."

"Sure," said Christopher. "Let's do it."

Johnny stepped into the living room. "Anyone for a cigar?" he asked them. "Cuban—only the best to celebrate Christopher's birthday!"

Joseph, Nonno, Pete, Jack, and a few other men Christopher recognized but had no idea what their names were, got up and came out onto the back deck with Johnny.

Johnny handed a cigar to everyone—including Christopher. He showed Christopher how to use the cigar cutter to cut one end, light it, and then take puffs that filled his mouth but not his lungs. Christopher coughed a little but quickly got the hang of it. Nonno had some advice, as did his father. Christopher felt like one of the guys, fully accepted into the family group as a man. This was cool.

He looked around to see if Michael was enjoying it too, but he wasn't there. He was still inside talking to Tony and Crystal. Although they were only partially visible through the sliding glass doors, it looked like the conversation was pretty deep. They were sitting at the kitchen counter. Tony had his head in his hands, then looked up smiling broadly. Crystal was smiling too, although she clearly had tears in her eyes. Christopher saw her wipe one away. What was that all about? He was about to go inside and find out, but Johnny put his hand on Christopher's arm, interrupting his thoughts.

"Isn't this nice, Christopher?" Johnny said. "It's what men do. We're bonding here." Everyone laughed.

Teresa opened the sliding doors and called them in. "The cake is ready. Time to sing happy birthday to our son, Joseph. Bring everyone in."

They put out their cigars and came into the kitchen. Teresa had moved the beverages to the counter and had placed a cake with sixteen lit candles in the center of the table. Joseph put his arm over Christopher's shoulders and brought him to stand near the cake as the guests sang "Happy Birthday."

Christopher didn't know what to wish for so he just blew out the candles. He really had everything already, didn't he?

"Presents! Presents! Presents!" Tony started the chanting in that obnoxious way he had, but everyone quickly joined in. They formed a Congo line with Christopher at the front and steered him into the living room. He sat in the wingback chair his grandfather had been in at the beginning of the party. Most of his relatives gave him money. He loved that. Momma had knitted him a sweater and put money in the pocket. His parents gave him a new computer and the application for his driving permit. He was very excited about driving. That was a cool thing to do for him. Tony and Crystal got him a video game that he was sure they would ask to come over and play with him. Next was Michael's gift.

Christopher unwrapped it slowly. It was pretty heavy. It felt like a textbook. Was Michael encouraging him to go to college? Giving him a head start? No. It wasn't a textbook. Christopher ran his hand over the soft leather. It was a Bible. His name was stamped in gold on the cover.

"A...Bible?" Christopher didn't know what to say. "Thanks, Michael. I think I still have one from when I was like thirteen, but this one is great. Thanks."

"Maybe you'll read this one?" Michael asked quietly.

"Yeah, sure. I will. I will read this one. Thanks." Christopher put it aside and reached for the last present, the one from Johnny.

Christopher wasn't careful with the wrapping on this one. He ripped it off quickly and opened the little box.

"Keys?" Christopher asked, puzzled. "You gave me keys?" He held them up.

"Yep." Johnny was grinning.

Christopher looked at the keys and then looked back at Johnny.

"No! No way! You got me the car? These are car keys? To the Mustang?"

"Yep." Johnny repeated, still grinning. "We'll go pick it up after you get your driver's permit."

"Oh my GOD! This is the best present…." Christopher caught himself as he looked around the room. "You all gave me the best presents ever! Thank you all so much!" He went around the room, shaking hands with the men and kissing the women. He hugged Johnny.

CHAPTER 16

Christopher loved his car. He drove it to school every day during his junior and senior year of high school. Sometimes he would feel sorry for Tony walking to school from across town and pick him up. They weren't exactly best friends but Christopher had learned to tolerate him and even sometimes enjoy his quirkiness, although he would never admit that to his "cool" friends.

Tony was no longer on the fencing team so Christopher didn't see him after school much. Fencing practice was mandatory five days a week. Tony had a job after school to help out his family so that pretty much nixed any extracurricular activities for him. They didn't have any classes in common either. Michael wasn't teaching carpentry anymore so Christopher had dropped that. He found he didn't like it as much as he had at first, and his father was insisting he go to college for pre-law so there were other classes now that were much more important. He needed to graduate at the top of his class so studying was a priority. Studying and cars, that is.

Most kids in his school had cars of their own, but they weren't vintage Mustangs. It kind of made him stick out—in a good way, of course. There were always a few girls hanging around him, asking for rides or admiring the color of the car. He kept it in pristine condition. His father would sometimes help him wash and wax it on Saturday mornings. They didn't talk much, but just hanging out with his dad was sort of cool. He thought maybe his dad secretly liked Mustangs as much as he did, although his father drove a Lexus. As far back as he could remember, his dad had driven luxury cars, not sporty ones. Christopher promised himself he would never switch to an "old person" car even after he was a rich lawyer. He might add a car a two, but this Mustang would be his favorite one forever.

This was finals week. He only had three, thankfully. His first exam started in 30 minutes and his last two were tomorrow. Christopher was sure he would ace them all, so he wasn't stressed out like some of the other students. Senior exams weren't as difficult as the state exams in his junior year had been. He couldn't wrap his head around the idea that high school would be over in one week. One week! Yikes!

His parents were planning another party for him. Christopher thought it was just another excuse to collect money from family and friends that would help him pay for college—or whatever he wanted. Christopher thought it might be nice to take a year off and do nothing, but he didn't dare say that to his mom or dad. They would absolutely freak out if they even had a hint of what he really wanted to do. Nothing. Just nothing. Didn't he deserve that? He had worked hard to please everyone since he was little. Now should be his time.

He pulled into the student parking lot and opened his car door. As he was getting out, he heard Johnny's voice, very loud and right next to his ear.

"Hey there almost-graduate!"

"Really? That was right in my ear! Where did you come from?" Christopher asked, putting a finger in his left ear.

"I've been here all along. You just didn't notice because you were so deep in thought." Johnny pointed to his Corvette parked nearby. "Ready for your exam?"

"I'm so ready," replied Christopher. "I just want this year to be over so I can..."

"Go to college?" Johnny finished for him. "Is that really what you want?"

Christopher paused. He was pretty sure Johnny would not say anything to his parents but just to be sure he asked him.

"Promise you won't say anything to Mom and Dad?"

"Sure kid. What's up?"

"I want to take a year off and just do my own thing. I don't know if I'm ready for college yet. More studying for at least four years? I need a break!"

Johnny smiled. "College is not all about studying, Chris. It is about freedom and experimentation and independence. You get to do what you want when you want it. If you stay home, your mom and dad will be watching everything you do and telling you what to do, just like they do now."

"I hadn't thought about that," Christopher considered.

"Just think—no curfews, no rules, no one watching…" Johnny let that sink in.

"You make it sound… fun."

"Oh, it is, believe me! And, I'm going back to college to pick up a few classes, so I'll make sure you have fun."

"What? You're going to be there too? That is so cool. Can we be roommates?"

"Nah. I'll live off campus. But don't worry," Johnny said quickly as Christopher's face fell, "You'll have so much fun living in a dorm with other guys…and girls." Johnny's eyes sparkled.

"Girls? Girls live in the dorm too?" Christopher was shocked and excited. "With the guys?"

"Yep. It's like living in an apartment building. You might have girls as neighbors."

"Cool," said Christopher.

"Best get to your exam," laughed Johnny. "You don't want to be late."

"Right. Thanks, Johnny." Christopher shut his car door and ran up the steps of the school.

"What are you doing?" Michael had parked his Jeep and seen Johnny talking to Christopher. He had noticed Johnny's subtle, conniving expressions during that conversation even though Christopher had appeared to miss them entirely.

"None of your business," replied Johnny.

"It is my business. I am supposed to protect him, and you seem intent to get in the way."

"Well, as a 'protector' you seem to be gone an awful lot. Some protector you are. Just leave him to me."

"No. You know I can't do that. Now, what's going on?"

"We were just talking about college. Christopher didn't want to go and I talked him into it."

"You did?" Michael was surprised. "You were persuading him to go to college? Why? I thought you would try to keep him from pursuing a career so he would become a deadbeat or something."

"Ha ha ha. Very funny." Johnny was not amused. "Of course I want what is best for him," he lied. "And I'm sure you'll agree that college is what is best for our little man."

"The absolute best thing is for him to meet and know our father, but college could be a good start," Michael admitted. "Maybe he'll meet him there."

"Maybe…or maybe not." Johnny's defiance showed on his face.

"You can't keep him from our father if he wants to meet him." Michael was adamant.

"Try me," Johnny snarled, turning away. He got in his Corvette and sped out of the parking lot.

CHAPTER 17

Summer was a blur of activity. Until, on the morning of August 14, just two weeks before college classes started, Momma died. She just sat down in her chair in the house where she and Nonno had lived for 65 years and died. No fuss. No complaining. No warning. Nonno found her there when she wouldn't answer his calls for coffee.

Nonno had his coffee cup in his hand as he shuffled into the room, looking for her. He called to her from across the room and, when she didn't answer, he went closer and saw that her skin was a mottled shade of grayish-blue. Her eyes were closed and her mouth gaped open.

"Momma! This is no joke. I'm out of coffee." Nonno shook her gently. "Wake up. Is this your way of getting out of getting me coffee?" A tear rolled down Nonno's cheek. "OK, then, Momma. You win." He put his coffee cup on the side table near her chair and stroked her hair. "You sleep in peace. God rest your soul."

Nonno picked up the phone and dialed Joseph.

"Joseph? Your mother's gone," he said when Joseph picked up the phone.

"Gone? Where'd she go?" Joseph asked.

"To Heaven, I hope," Nonno replied. "Just up and died without telling me. Found her just sitting in her chair."

"Did you call an ambulance, Pop?" asked Joseph.

"No I did not." Nonno said. "What are they going to do for her now, Joseph? I'll call my cousin Vincent."

"Pop, it's not like that. I'll take care of everything. You just sit down and relax. We'll be over there soon."

"I'll sit, but I don't have my coffee. She didn't make my coffee," Nonno said.

"I'll bring you coffee, Pop. We'll be there in ten minutes."

"OK. OK. You're a good boy." Nonno sounded a little out of it as Joseph hung up the phone.

"Teresa!" Joseph shouted for his wife. "Christopher!"

"What is it?" They both came running. Joseph's voice had been loud but shaky. He had a handkerchief out and was wiping his eyes.

"Momma's gone. She passed." Joseph choked back a sob. "My Momma's gone."

Teresa gave him a hug, then motioned to include Christopher in the embrace.

"Let's go," she said. "Nonno will need us." She dialed 9-1-1 on her cell phone as she walked back to the kitchen and poured some coffee in a to-go cup for Nonno, with two sugars and a dash of cream, just like he liked it.

"Hello, what is your emergency?" a voice asked on the other end of the line. Teresa explained what had happened and gave the dispatcher the address.

Christopher and his father were in the car waiting as Teresa came out and got in. They drove in silence, none of them saying a word until they pulled up to Nonno's front door and got out of the car.

Nonno came outside to greet them. Teresa gave him the coffee.

"It's in a paper cup," he said, displeased. "The coffee doesn't taste the same in a paper cup."

"It's all right, Nonno," said Teresa. "Let's go inside and I'll pour it into one of your coffee mugs."

"You're a good girl, Teresa," said Nonno, patting her cheek. "Come on in and say hi to Momma…" His voice trailed off. "Well, you can see her anyway." He led the way back into the house, stopping at the living room door and pointing to the chair where Momma sat so still and quiet.

It was eerie seeing her there, like that. No breath sounds. No movement. Christopher backed up. He didn't want to see her like this. Teresa went into the kitchen and poured the coffee into Nonno's favorite mug and gave it to him. She came back to the doorway where the others were standing, just looking into the room.

Teresa gave Joseph and Christopher a little push from behind and they went into the room, making the sign of the cross over their hearts. Joseph knelt in front of the chair and took Momma's hands in his.

"Momma!" he sobbed. "We are going to miss you so much."

Teresa put her hand on Joseph's shoulder, trying to comfort him. Nonno shuffled in and sat down in his chair, opposite Momma, coffee in hand. He sipped it and sighed. "This is almost as good as Momma makes," he said. "Almost… as… good…as…"

Christopher, Teresa, and Joseph turned around as Nonno's voice trailed off and his fingers slowly released his grip on the cup. It fell to the floor, shattering into hundreds of pieces and spilling the hot liquid on his stocking feet. They expected him to cry out or curse but he didn't. He just closed his eyes and stopped breathing.

The doorbell rang as Teresa screamed.

Christopher saw the red lights of the ambulance flashing through the window as he answered the door. He pointed into the living room and stepped aside as the paramedics came through the front door carrying large medical bags. For a moment, they didn't know what to do first. Two elderly people sat in chairs, obviously deceased. A woman lay on the ground, face down with a man kneeling and bending over her, shaking her and sobbing.

"What happened? A paramedic turned to Christopher, hoping to get some clues.

"Uh, uh, uh…" Christopher was finding it difficult to form words of any kind. He just stood and pointed, first at Momma, then Nonno, then to his mother on the floor. To his relief, Teresa moaned and rolled over.

"My mom… my mom fainted, I think," Christopher said. "My grandmother died in her chair, and my grandfather called to tell us, and so we came ,and then he died too, and my mom fainted." Christopher ran out of breath as the paramedic knelt to examine Teresa.

"Ma'am, can you hear me?" he asked her, reaching to take her pulse and motioning for Joseph to move out of the way.

Teresa groaned and tried to sit up. "Yes. Yes. I'm all right, I think." Her voice was weak. "I just fainted. It was a shock to be here when Nonno—that's my father-in-law—passed away. I'm fine." She tried to push his hand away but he held on tightly to her wrist.

"We're just going to check you out to be sure," he told her firmly but kindly. "Two deaths today is enough."

Teresa went limp and began crying. She let him finish his exam. When he told her that her blood pressure and pulse were fine, but she should probably go to the hospital anyway to be checked out, Teresa refused.

"No. I need to be here for my family." The color was back in her face and she was feeling much better. "Joseph, please help me up."

Joseph took her hands and helped her to her feet. He wrapped his arms around her in a big hug and they cried together as the paramedics put Nonno and Momma on stretchers and loaded them into the ambulance.

"We're taking them to the hospital morgue where a doctor will certify their deaths. You can have your funeral director call to make arrangements." A paramedic explained the process to Teresa and Joseph. They nodded and kept their arms tightly around each other.

Christopher stepped back out of the way as the stretchers came through the doorway. He didn't know what to say or do. How can life change so suddenly? In what seemed like an instant he had lost both grandparents. What would Sunday dinners be like now? Who would he go to for help when someone tried to bully him at college? Would this impact the power and influence the D'Antoni's had with their patriarch gone? Who was he without his grandmother and grandfather? He had thought they would always be there. He had never thought of them not being there for him or of them actually dying.

Christopher shivered. This was the first time he had actually seen death. Sure, Billy had died, but he deserved it, and Christopher hadn't seen it so he could put it out of his mind. He had seen Nonno slip away. He had seen Momma's dead face. He was pretty sure both would haunt him forever. This was not right. This was not fair. He ran into the bathroom and threw up.

CHAPTER 18

I t seemed like everyone was at the funeral. It was standing
room only in the enormous Catholic church. Nonno and
Momma had known a lot of people. Christopher was seated
with his mother and father in the front pew. It had been
years since he had been in this church. Father Giovanni
was not here anymore. Christopher briefly wondered what
had happened to him. Had he died too? It was a young
priest now that was going on and on about death and life
after death and Christ and giving Communion. What the
heck did he know about death? He could not have been
that much older than Johnny or Michael. No life experience.
Unbelievable. Really. Not believable at all.

Christopher looked around for Johnny and Michael
and wondered why they weren't there. He hadn't told them
about Momma and Nonno, but they seemed to always know
everything before everyone else, so he had not thought it
necessary to call them. In fact, he purposefully didn't call
them. He couldn't call them. He couldn't talk about it. If they
loved his family as much as they said they did, they should
just know. The fact that they weren't here, it just showed…
it just showed…well, something.

Christopher hadn't cried. He felt like he had to hold it together for his parents. They were crying all the time. The priest talked about "hope in the life hereafter." It sure didn't look like his parents had hope in the life hereafter by the way they were sobbing. Christopher believed them over the priest. They would know. Nonno and Momma were just gone. Life was over and there was no more. That was depressing in one way but comforting in another. If there was no life after death, then there was no Heaven, but there was also no Hell. Christopher figured if the truth got out the priest would have no job. No wonder he was droning on and on about it.

Christopher shifted in his seat and looked at his watch. His mother frowned at him in the corrective way only she could do. He sat up and looked straight ahead for the rest of the service.

Finally, the organist began playing "Ave Maria" and the congregation stood up to watch the pallbearers carry the caskets out of the church with the family walking out after them. Teresa, Joseph, and Christopher got into the limo and headed toward the cemetery. Christopher stared out the window of the limo. He had nothing to say. He just watched the long line of cars with their headlights on following along behind them.

When they got to the cemetery, Teresa was the first to notice Johnny and Michael standing near the gravesite.

"Look, Christopher! Johnny and Michael came!" She seemed pleased.

Christopher looked. He didn't know if he was pleased or not. Michael would talk about Heaven and Johnny would try to make him laugh and forget about being sad. He wasn't sure he wanted either of those things right now.

They got out of the limo. Teresa went up to Johnny and Michael and gave each of them a hug. "Thank you, boys, for being here. You've been a part of our family for so long. You must be sad too."

"We are, Mom," said Johnny. Teresa smiled at the "mom."

"We are so sad," Johnny continued. "Nonno and Momma were like our grandpa and grandma too. We don't have grandparents, so they were extra special to us."

Michael, as always the quieter of the two, just gave Teresa and Joseph a hug without saying anything.

Christopher stood there, eyes down.

"Hey buddy. How are you doing?" Michael asked him.

"Fine, I guess," Christopher replied, shrugging.

"Well, I'm here for you," said Michael.

"Yeah, I know. Thanks," said Christopher.

Michael and Christopher stood in silence side by side a short distance away looking at the two large holes in the ground where the caskets would go. Johnny was still with Teresa and Joseph, receiving condolences as if he was actually their son. In fact, he received more condolences than Christopher did. That annoyed Christopher a little. Of course, he was standing outside the family circle, so perhaps they didn't notice him. He decided he was really was OK with that. Right now he didn't want to be noticed or told how sorry people were for him. Michael seemed to know that. How did he know that? He just stood quietly next to him without saying a word, and somehow that comforted Christopher more than anything else had.

Christopher listened to the voices around him—his Aunt Fanny and mother talking about the makeup artist who had made his grandmother look like she was still alive but sleeping, Uncle Jack discussing the cut of Nonno's burial suit, cousins wondering what the headstones would look like, and everyone saying how good and perfect Nonno and Momma had been. Christopher knew better. He had been like a shadow when he was little, listening from the other rooms as his grandfather had ordered the executions of his competition and of those who had crossed him. You don't grow up in a mob family without witnessing some really bad things, but he had never said a word about what he had heard or seen to anyone. After all, if you ignore the bad things, you can convince yourself they never happened. At first he had thought lightening would strike Nonno dead because of what he was doing, just like the priest said in church. But, instead, Nonno had grown wealthier and more powerful and died an old man. That must mean God approved, right? That is, if there was a God. Christopher sighed. It was all so confusing.

"Michael, do you believe there is a God?" Christopher asked him.

"I don't only believe it, Christopher, I know it to be true," Michael replied.

"And a Heaven? If there's a God, there must be a Heaven, right?" Christopher continued.

"Yes, there is definitely a Heaven," Michael said wistfully. "It's beautiful…"

Christopher raised an eyebrow and looked at him quizzically. "How do you know for sure? Do you think Nonno and Momma are there?"

Michael looked sad. "The only way people can get into Heaven after they die is if they believe that Jesus is the one true God, they believe that Jesus died for them and that He rose from the dead, they repent of their sin, and they make a commitment to live in obedience to Jesus. Once they truly believe and have made that promise to God, He writes their name in the Book of Life. Their soul is freed from the grip Satan has on it and is welcomed to Heaven when it leaves the body. It's pretty awesome."

"And if a person doesn't do that? Where do they go when they die?"

"A person who does not belong to Jesus goes to Hell."

"Wow. That was blunt, Michael," said Christopher, offended. "And really mean. I can't believe that. If there is a God, and I'm really not sure about that right now, He couldn't possibly send people to Hell. He's supposed to love everyone, right?"

"Hell was not created for people," Michael explained. "It was created for Satan and his angels. But, if a person does not get free from Satan's grip during their lifetime, they are dragged down to Hell by him when they die. Satan is angry at God and will take as many of God's children to Hell with him as he can in order to get back at God. To answer your other question, Christopher, God does love everyone. That's why He provided a way for people to escape. But everyone has to make that choice on their own. A loving God won't force anyone to love Him."

"But how did that even happen? Why would a loving God let Satan get a grip in the first place? Why didn't He protect us?" Christopher argued.

"Humans were created in the image of God, with free will, so that they could walk and talk with Him and enjoy just being with Him. Unfortunately, Adam and Eve made the choice to listen to Satan instead of God. This gave Satan that grip on their souls which they passed along to all of their descendants. God warned them but they didn't listen. A loving God won't force anyone to obey Him either. It is a choice all humans have. A loving God gave you a choice."

Christopher shook his head. "Sorry I asked." This made no sense to him. It seemed just like more of the mumbo-jumbo the priest talked about.

"I'm not sorry you asked. I've been waiting for you to ask." Michael smiled. "You are important to God, and I know…"

"Christopher!" Johnny interrupted their conversation. "Hey, sorry I was not here with you right away. Your mom and dad seemed to need me for a bit, but I'm here with you now. How are you doing?"

"Just great." Christopher's tone was sarcastic. "Michael just told me my Nonno and Momma are in Hell."

Michael's face fell. "Christopher…"

"Nah, that's OK. I don't believe in Heaven or Hell or God or Satan, so go ahead and say whatever you want. Let's go, Johnny. I don't want to be here anymore." Christopher turned and walked away.

Johnny gave a look of triumph and followed Christopher out of the cemetery. He gave a little wave and said loud enough for only Michael to hear, "See you later, loser."

Michael felt the familiar flush of temper he often experienced around Johnny, but he let it go. "It's not over yet, Johnny," he said to the air.

CHAPTER 19

College seemed to be everything Johnny had told him it would be. Christopher settled in the dorms at Vassar and made friends quickly, especially when they found out his last name was D'Antoni. His father had taken over the family business and was just as efficient as Nonno had been in keeping things running smoothly. They had a reputation that was, so far, unchallenged, even this far north of New York City in the middle of Dutchess County.

Christopher's roommate was Timothy James Rupert, or TJ for short. He was at Vassar on scholarship because he was a genius or something—that was the rumor anyway. Christopher hadn't asked him yet. They were still getting to know each other. TJ was from North Carolina and had a southern drawl that the girls found charming. The "hey sugar" and the "all y'alls" were a little much in Christopher's opinion, but what the heck, if it brought the girls to their table during meals and when they walked on the Common, he would deal with it.

The parties and girls were the best part of college, but Christopher did enjoy his classes too. He had signed up for a variety of courses that interested him since Vassar didn't have a pre-law curriculum per se. He loved the intellectual discussions in his Constitutional Law class, so maybe his father was right. Maybe law was the best field for him to be in. He had found he had a knack for arguing until his opponent—or his friends—conceded his point. Handy skill to have if he would take over the family business one day, right? He could intimidate with words rather than muscle.

Christopher knew he might have to back off on the arguing, though, at least with his friends. One night TJ had told him he was being an ass. Wow. Christopher guessed TJ's southern charm was reserved for the females because he certainly wasn't getting any of it. He had almost—almost— punched TJ in the nose for that comment. He wasn't sure what held him back but he was later glad he hadn't done it. He found out after another freshman got in the way of TJ's fist during the same frat party that TJ had been on his high school's boxing team. Christopher liked his pretty-boy face just the way it was. He did not need a broken jaw or a crooked nose. Thank goodness he had just laughed off TJ's comment that night and walked away. An intoxicated TJ was an angry, aggressive TJ. He would avoid drunk TJ in the future.

It was Friday night and perfect late-September weather for an outdoor party in the park across the road from the dorms. Johnny had said he would be there. Christopher hadn't seen Johnny much since he'd been here, but that had actually been OK. His new friends were just as fun.

At around 9:00 p.m. Christopher could hear the music from his dorm window.

"Come on, TJ, let's go to the party," Christopher said grabbing his jacket. "It sounds like we're missing out on some of the fun!"

"Just a sec," TJ said, shutting his laptop. "I've got to get some…supplies." TJ opened his top dresser drawer and put his hand all the way to the back, rummaging through the clothes. "Ah, here they are." He kissed the small ziplock bag containing a handful of pills that he held between two fingers. "Gotta make some money to take my girls out in style," he said grinning.

"What are you doing?" Christopher asked in surprise. "What are those?"

"These?" TJ said, still grinning and holding up the baggie. "They are easy money, my boy. Really easy money."

"Where did you get them?"

"Do you really think I'm going to give up the name of my supplier? So you can undersell me? No way! If you want to sell, you'll need to find your own supplier. However…if you want to buy…" he teased, "I'm your man."

"Nope. Not for me," said Christopher. "But you do what you want. You'll get no judgment from me. Let's go."

The two freshmen left their room, locking the door behind them, and joined the crowd of students headed toward the park.

Once they got there, Christopher looked around for Johnny. It would be hard to miss his six-foot-two-inch friend in this crowd. If he didn't see him, he would hear him. Johnny's laugh was unmistakeable. It made everyone around him laugh too and relax. It was hypnotic, in a way. All the bad things in the world disappeared when Johnny laughed with you. He liked that.

"Having fun yet?" Johnny's voice was next to his ear. Good thing, too, because the party was getting loud.

"Hi Johnny. We just got here. This is my roommate TJ." Christopher introduced them.

Johnny eyed TJ warily, then relaxed and laughed. "I thought you might not be the sort I want my brother here to hang out with, but I see you are perfect—just perfect! What's that in your pocket?" He pointed to the shirt pocket where TJ had stuffed the drugs.

"Molly. You in the market for some?"

"Maybe. Is it mixed with anything?"

"Nah. Just straight Molly."

"Johnny," Christopher interrupted, "You can't seriously be thinking about taking this stuff."

"Not for me, young man. You are right. It's not the thing for me." He winked at TJ and slipped him a $50 bill without Christopher noticing. "Right, TJ? You understand? It's not my thing."

TJ's genius mind was quick. He understood. "Sure, Johnny. I got it. Not your scene. Thanks." He quickly put the money in his back pants pocket.

"Great. Great. Let's go get some beer." Johnny led the three of them to the kegs at the far side of the field.

Beer Christopher would do. Beer was harmless. He just knew to only have a couple. When he felt the buzz, he stopped drinking. If TJ had too many beers and got out of hand, Christopher would just go hang out with his other friends. He was still afraid of getting into trouble and disappointing his mom. His dad would probably be delighted, but his mom—no. He would someday have to get away from the "be a good boy" mentality ingrained in him since he was a baby. Maybe tonight! Maybe he would get drunk for once. Johnny was here. He wouldn't let it go too far so, hey, why not? Christopher was satisfied with his internal argument and was ready to party.

TJ stepped up and poured a drink for Johnny, handing it to him. He slipped the contents of one of the capsules into the bottom of the next red party cup before filling it. Christopher did not see him do it and took the beer, turning to talk to Johnny as TJ got the last beer for himself.

The three of them walked back through the crowd to the gazebo. The DJ was playing all of the latest music and several students were already dancing and swaying to the beat, red beer cups held high in the air.

Johnny and TJ walked ahead of Christopher, talking animatedly. Geez, you'd think they were best friends! But Christopher knew Johnny was like that. He could make friends with anyone in an instant. He was so friendly and nice. Everyone liked him.

Christopher found it difficult to walk through the crowded park without bumping into people. He certainly couldn't enjoy his beer until they found a quieter spot. He planned to drink and observe the girls for a bit. Check out his choices. The beer would give him courage to ask the prettiest girls to dance and maybe even go out with him. He was about to call ahead to Johnny and TJ to wait for him, but before he could shout to them over the noise, someone bumped into him from behind so hard that his full cup of beer spilled down the front of his shirt and onto the ground.

"Oh shit!" Christopher couldn't help the expletive. He crumpled the cup and threw it to the ground in disgust.

"Sorry, man." The voice sounded familiar.

"Tony? What the hell?" Christopher was angry.

"Sorry, Chris. I didn't see you. Honest! It's just so crowded here. I'll get you another drink. You know they're free, right? Sorry."

"What are you doing here?" Christopher demanded to know. "This is a party for Vassar students only. You're going to the Community College," he said with disdain.

"I'm with Crystal. She...she's a student here." Tony turned around in a circle. "She's here somewhere."

"Never mind. I don't care. I have to go change. I'm outta here."

"Sorry!" Tony called out again as Christopher walked away.

"Hi Tony." Johnny had come back to find Christopher. "Where's Christopher going?"

"Oh, I knocked into him—by accident, I swear! And his beer spilled down his shirt. He's super mad at me because I don't think he even got to take one sip of it. I told him I'd get him another one but he just left. Crystal will be sad she didn't get to say hi. She's here somewhere." Tony did another little twirl visually scanning the area for Crystal. He stopped short when he saw the angry scowl on Johnny's face.

Johnny glared at Tony. His perfect plan ruined by this jerk. Wait! There was something different about Tony. His braces were off now. His acne was almost gone. His hair was combed. His clothes were actually decent and clean. But all of that didn't add up to the changed vibe Johnny was getting from him. What was it? All of a sudden it clicked.

"Have you been talking to Michael?" Johnny asked Tony.

"Uh, yeah. We talk all the time. Why?" Tony was puzzled. "Was he supposed to tell me something?"

"No. No he was not. I just wondered what you guys have been talking about."

"Well, that's nosy," Tony said. "Why do you want to know?"

"There's something different about you—something off about you." Johnny couldn't come right out and ask. He was pretty sure what it was. He had seen this a few times before, but he would have to get Tony to tell him on his own and then hope he could mask his reaction when he did.

Tony smiled. "You noticed? Wow. That means it's real."

Johnny nodded impatiently. "Go on…"

"Well, we've been talking a lot about God and Jesus and stuff in the Bible."

Johnny flinched as if in pain.

Tony continued, "I believe all of it. I asked Jesus to be my savior. I did it! I'm saved now! And Crystal did too. Isn't that great?"

"Hmmm," grunted Johnny. It was too late now for this one and for the girl. He hadn't seen it coming. He had been too wrapped up in Christopher. Had he gotten things wrong?

"Great. Just great." Johnny didn't sound all that happy to Tony. "Let's go get that beer."

"Oh, no thanks, Johnny. I've got to find Crystal. See you!" Tony gave Johnny a fist bump and pushed his way back through the crowd, disappearing from sight.

Johnny was too angry for words but he wasn't wasting a night like this. He had lost rounds one and two, which he didn't even know they were playing, but he would not lose round three—the important one, the decisive one.

"Hey TJ! My man!" Johnny held up a hand and waved TJ over.

TJ couldn't stop jumping up and down to the music, even as he made his way over to Johnny. He bobbed his head back and forth, up and down as he jumped and wiggled all over. He had one arm wrapped around a girl's shoulders. She was stumbling along side of TJ, obviously wasted— with drugs or booze, Johnny couldn't tell. It didn't really matter. TJ was high too, so he probably wouldn't remember anything in the morning.

"Your roommate went back to the dorm," Johnny told him.

"OK. No prob," said TJ. "We'll go to your room, right sweetheart?"

"Wait! I need you to do me a favor before you two get comfy," Johnny interrupted. "Do you have any more Mollies?"

"Nope. Sold 'em all. I can get more tomorrow. Y'all will have to wait til then. Sorry bud." TJ and his girl bounced away.

The words Johnny screamed in his mind were too appalling for anyone to hear.

CHAPTER 20

In the morning, Christopher woke to find TJ sprawled face down on the floor by his bed. He gave him a nudge with his foot.

"Hey, TJ, you OK?" he asked.

TJ moaned and rolled over, covering his eyes with his arms.

"What time is it?"

"What happened?" Christopher ignored TJ's question and asked his own. He figured knowing his roommate was OK was better than knowing what time it was.

"Well, I didn't get lucky, as y'all can see." TJ sat up. "I had a girl all primed and ready, but we had to go to her room, because you were acting like a baby crying over spilled beer. What a loser!" he joked.

"Shut up." Christopher was in no mood for this. "Why are you on the floor?"

"I don't know, buddy. After Melissa's or Elsa's or whatever her name is's roommate wouldn't let me in their room, I came back here. I don't remember much after leaving that room. I guess I was just too tired to get into bed."

"Too tired or too wasted?" Christopher asked him.

TJ smiled. "You choose."

Christopher helped TJ to his feet. "You need a shower."

TJ sniffed his armpits and grinned. "Yep. I sure do."

"I can't believe you thought you were having fun! You can't even remember it." Christopher had to get the last word. He had to be right.

TJ shrugged, still grinning. "Don't knock it til you've tried it," he said as he left the room, heading for the showers.

Christopher threw on his clothes, tied his sneakers, and grabbed his jacket and cell phone on the way out of the dorm room. He stuck a piece of gum in his mouth and started chewing. It was the same as brushing your teeth, right? At least on this Saturday morning it would have to do. He needed to find Johnny and apologize for deserting him last night. He pulled his cell phone out of his back pocket and called him.

"Hey, Johnny. It's me. Are you awake yet? Can we talk about last night?"

Johnny laughed in that charming way he had, putting Christopher at ease. "Sure, man. Where are you? I'll pick you up and we can go get breakfast. I'm starving! No worries, though, about last night, I mean. It's cool."

"I'm at the College Avenue entrance. I didn't know how to find you."

"No problem. I'll be there in a few minutes. I'm not far."

True to his word, Johnny pulled up in his Corvette just a few minutes later. "Hop in!" he told Christopher, reaching over and pushing open the car door.

Christopher spit his gum in the grass and got in the car.

"I'm sorry I bailed on you last night," he told Johnny. "Tony came with Crystal and the jerk bumped into me and spilled beer down the front of my shirt. It was sticky and disgusting."

Johnny glanced sideways at Christopher. "And that's what made you run back to the dorm and stay there?"

Christopher was quiet for a minute before he answered. "No. Not really. I mean, I was mad at Tony for making the mess, but, I guess it was more that I didn't want to see Crystal and I needed to get out of there before she saw me or I saw her. I didn't know she was a student here. We haven't talked since my birthday party last year."

"Oh, sorry—I thought you said you didn't want to see Crystal when you really meant you did want to see her," Johnny teased.

"I don't know what I want," said Christopher. "But anyway, she picked Tony over me, so that's that."

"Maybe she just looks good to you because you can't have her," Johnny suggested. "It's always the forbidden fruit that tastes the sweetest."

"Maybe." Christopher hoped that was all it was. He had thought he had put her out of his mind and was moving on, but now she was here.

"I know just the thing to cure you of your melancholy," Johnny said. "Let's pick up a couple of girls and head into Poughkeepsie. We can rent kayaks and go out on the river. It'll be fun and take your mind off of you-know-who."

"Yeah. Sounds great," said Christopher. "I know where we're getting the kayaks, but where are we getting the girls?"

"Right here." Johnny pulled into a parking spot at the Palace Diner. He pointed to two very attractive college women walking up the steps to the front door of the diner. One was blonde and petite. She had a dimple in her cheek that accented her cute smile. Her hair fell in loose curls around her face and down her shoulders. The tight t-shirt she was wearing left little to the imagination, showing off her cleavage and the curve of her breasts. Her jeans were tight, too, outlining parts of her body Christopher thought he shouldn't be looking so closely at.

The other girl was taller and dark-haired. She had an athletic build, with long legs and lean arms. She was wearing a midriff top and low cut jeans, showing off a small gold ring in her belly button. Her eyes were large and round, a stunning bright blue like the waters of the Caribbean Sea. They reflected the laughter in her voice as she talked animatedly to her friend. They opened the door and disappeared inside the diner.

"Dibs on the tall one," said Johnny.

Christopher laughed. "I'll be happy to take your leftovers," he said.

Johnny and Christopher followed the women in. When the hostess saw them, she told them she was sorry, but they had no booths left. It would be about a half hour wait until something opened up. Johnny winked at Christopher and nodded toward the two women.

"We're with them," he told the hostess.

"Oh, OK. Follow me," she told them, leading them to the table where the women were sitting. She handed them menus and walked away.

"Hello ladies," said Johnny. "Sorry to intrude but there were no tables left and we were hoping we could share one with you." He put on his "melt their heart" smile and the women giggled.

"Of course," said the tall one. "I'm Sophia. This is my friend Emma."

"Charmed." Johnny made an exaggerated bow. "I'm Johnny and this is my friend Christopher. We are pleased to make your acquaintance."

Sophia laughed and rolled her eyes. "Sit down already!" She moved over to make room for Johnny.

Emma smiled at Christopher and patted the seat next to her. "And you may sit here," she said.

Christopher slid into the booth. He wasn't sure how it was going to go, but Emma and Sophia were easy to talk to and the conversation flowed as if the four of them had known each other forever. At the end of the meal Johnny invited them to go kayaking and the girls accepted enthusiastically.

They spent the rest of the morning on the Hudson River, paddling upstream and then back to the dock where they had rented the double kayaks. Christopher hardly noticed the scenery, except when Emma leaned forward and pointed out something she thought was beautiful or funny or unusual. He did notice how close she was to him, how she touched him gently on the shoulder when she was excited about something, and how her voice in his ear made him feel like kissing her. If they weren't both facing forward all day, maybe he would have kissed her already. He was wishing he had chosen the back seat so he could have watched her all day. Even if it was just the back of her head, that would have been fine. Instead, she had insisted he take the front, so she watched him all day. He wondered what she was thinking.

Uh oh! Christopher realized he hadn't showered that morning or combed his hair or, gulp, brushed his teeth. She was probably thinking he stunk. Oh wait, he had showered last night to wash the beer off. His hair was probably adorably tousled. She seemed to like it. He took out another piece of gum and popped it into his mouth. When Emma was looking off to the side, he blew into his hand and sniffed. Christopher sighed in relief. His breath was fine—a little minty actually. He was ready for that kiss now.

They paddled up to the dock just a little behind Sophia and Johnny. Johnny reached out a hand to help Emma out and then held the kayak steady for Christopher. None of them seemed ready to end their day yet. Sophia and Johnny were holding hands as they walked back to their cars.

Emma reached out and took Christopher's hand. "I hope this is OK," she said.

"Uh, yeah. It's great," Christopher told her, giving her hand a squeeze. He was feeling shy and thinking a lot about kissing her.

Emma's car was parked next to Johnny's. "Hey, why don't you come with me, Sophia," Johnny said. "I'll show you my place. Christopher can catch a ride with Emma."

Emma spoke up quickly. "That's OK with me." She was intrigued by this shy, handsome boy.

Sophia curled her arms around Johnny's neck. "I won't be coming home right away, OK, Emma?"

"Gotcha," said Emma. "Christopher, do you have anywhere you need to be?"

"No." Christopher accidentally swallowed his gum.

"Great!" Emma said. "Do you want to come over and hang out for a while?"

"I guess..." Christopher was absolutely sure he did. He would never admit this to anyone, not even Johnny, but he had not kissed a girl since Crystal. There had been many girls and dates but nothing serious enough or long enough to lead to kissing much less anything else. He was in college now and ready for some sexual experiences. Heck, yeah!

On the drive to Emma's apartment Christopher learned that she was a junior at Marist College, just down the road from where he went to school. She was only two years older than he was, she broke up with her boyfriend last week, and she was unsure what she wanted to do with her life. Christopher liked the way she confided in him. It made him feel...special again. He hadn't felt this way since elementary school when he was the "miracle boy" everyone loved—before the middle school bullying and the high school drama. He liked it. He liked it very much.

When they got to Emma's place, she took his hand and led him through the front door. When he paused at the living room, she giggled, took both his hands in hers and pulled him into her bedroom. She shut the door, stood on tip toes, and wrapped her arms around his neck.

"Kiss me, please," Emma said in a very sexy whisper, her lips just inches from his. Christopher did. And did again. And again. She tasted sweet and warm, like cinnamon rolls fresh from the oven. He did not want to stop, ever.

Christopher felt himself grow hard against her. Emma took his hands and put them on her breasts. He could feel the shape of her nipples through her t-shirt. He took a deep breath and found that he was really, really enjoying this moment. Second base on the first date. This was awesome. He felt like a college man now.

Just when he thought they should probably stop, Emma slipped out of her clothes and stood naked in front of him. Christopher didn't know what to do. He didn't know what to say. She reached out and pulled his shirt over his head, then reached down and unzipped his pants.

"You want this, right?" she asked him. "I want you, too. No strings attached. I find you very sexy, Chris. Let's do this."

"Umm…I've never…" Christopher was embarrassed now. Technically, he knew what to do, but practically, he had no idea.

Emma didn't laugh, as Christopher had feared she might. Instead, she just pulled him down onto the bed so they were lying side by side facing each other. "No worries," she said. "I'll teach you." Emma rolled onto her back. She took Christopher's hand and put it between her legs.

When Christopher got back to the dorm he was smiling and humming what he thought was a pretty jazzy tune. TJ wasn't around. The room was empty. Christopher was bursting. He had to tell someone. This was the most awesome day in his life so far, although getting his Mustang was a pretty close second.

His cell phone rang. "How was your date?" It was Johnny.

"The most awesome thing happened!" Chris was bursting with his news. "I did it. I mean we did it. We had sex!"

"That's awesome dude," laughed Johnny. "I thought you might. Congratulations!"

"How was your date?" Christopher asked Johnny. "Did you guys…you know…have sex?"

"What do you think?" asked Johnny.

"Totally. You totally did." Christopher said. "I mean, of course you did. You've probably had dozens of women by now."

"I'm proud of you, Chris," Johnny told him. "You've finally become a man."

"Yeah. Yeah! I can't wait to see her again."

"She didn't tell you?" Johnny asked.

"Tell me what?"

"They are studying abroad this semester. They leave tomorrow."

"No. No, Emma didn't tell me. Why wouldn't she tell me that?" Christopher was confused. He thought Emma really liked him.

"She gave you a gift. Sex with no strings attached. Just fun and a little bit of education, yes?"

"Yes, I guess," Christopher said slowly. "She did say something about no strings attached."

"See? There you go. A learning experience for you that broke the ice, so to speak, leaving you experienced and ready for all the other college women out there."

"But I really liked her, and I thought we..."

"What?" Johnny interrupted. "Were boyfriend and girlfriend after one date? Were madly in love? Would get married one day? That's ridiculous. It was just sex."

That stung a little. Christopher had felt like he was falling a little bit in love with Emma. It hadn't been just sex. It had been first sex. It seemed to him that first sex should be something special, but evidently it wasn't. It was just supposed to prepare him for next sex. Suddenly, he felt a little depressed. Johnny had burst his happiness bubble. Or was it really Emma who had done that?

"Buddy, you still there?" Johnny sensed the change of mood when Christopher stopped talking. "Hello?"

"I've gotta go. I've got studying to do." Christopher ended the phone call and sat down on his bed.

"College sucks," he thought. Christopher wanted to talk to someone who wasn't fake. The girls had known what they were doing, and they hadn't been truthful. At first, Christopher thought he and Johnny might be taking advantage of the girls, but he realized with a start that it had been completely the other way around—at least for him.

He flipped through the contacts on his phone and paused over Crystal's name. What the heck, he thought, and dialed her number.

When Crystal didn't answer, Christopher tried Tony's number. While it rang, Christopher wondered why he had thought Tony would be a good choice as a confidant. They hadn't talked in almost a year, except for at the party where Tony had almost knocked him down. The words they had exchanged there had not been friendly, at least the ones he had spoken.

Christopher hung up and threw his phone on the bed. What was he doing? Johnny was right. Sex was just part of the college experience. He would enjoy it for what it was. He had gotten played this time. He would not let that happen again.

Chapter 21

Michael tried to visit Christopher at college a few times, but it didn't go well. The easy relationship they had enjoyed in the past seemed to have slipped away this year. Christopher wasn't sure why, except that he felt Michael disapproved of his new lifestyle. Christopher was becoming more and more like Johnny and TJ, learning how to put on the charm and use his smile and handsome face to get whatever he wanted. The grades were slipping a bit, but he was still passing all of his classes with at least a 3.0, and his parents were happy about that. Michael thought he could do better. Christopher felt it was unreasonable to expect him to study more than he was doing now. He could earn higher grades, sure, but why was it necessary? He needed to have fun, too. Right?

He and TJ used the "sock on the door" sign when they had girls in the room. When Christopher saw the sock, he would go to the library for an hour or take a girl to the burger joint a few blocks away. It never took TJ more than an hour and then the room was ready for Christopher to use with his date.

TJ's drug business expanded to include condom sales and Christopher took advantage of that part of it. A guy had to be careful. His parents would freak out if he got a girl pregnant, although he was pretty sure his dad would take care of things if that happened. Pretty sure, and a little afraid.

On the Sunday before second semester finals, Christopher planned to hang out with Johnny and TJ. They were all taking a break from girls and studying. TJ had suggested hiking up to the southern peak of Mount Beacon. He had done it once before and said the view was amazing. He told them they could see New York City from the lookout tower there.

They three young men threw their hiking gear into the back of TJ's truck. They each had a backpack with water, a knife, a compass, and a first aid kit. TJ's backpack included beer and an assortment of drugs as well.

TJ shrugged when Christopher noticed that and told him, "Be prepared—that's my motto. Don't you worry. I'll have you or Johnny drive the truck back if I'm high. Yer safe, buddy. No problem. Right?"

Christopher just turned away and got into the truck's back seat. Johnny pretended not to hear and got in the front seat. TJ hopped in the driver's seat and bellowed, "Let's get started on this here adventure!"

It took about 45 minutes to reach the parking area at the base of the mountain. They got out of the truck, grabbed their backpacks, and headed up the stairs to the trail that started just to the left of an old, deserted incline railway.

After about a mile almost straight up on the steep, rocky trail, there was a flat overlook where they stopped for a rest and a drink of water. It was beautiful. They could see the Hudson River winding its way through the valley for miles. Johnny jumped up on a rock and gestured grandly around him. "All this could be yours if the price is right!" he said in a dramatic, game-show host voice.

TJ laughed and opened a beer. "All this is ours anyway," he said. "Look around you. No one else is here!"

Johnny jumped down from the rock. "That's what you think," he said. "There have been people here." He pointed out the glass from broken bottles, the cigarette butts, the used condoms, and the McDonald's hamburger wrappers littering the ground around them.

"OK, OK, so people have fun here. Let's move along. I'm guessing this is where the partying happens and people don't go any higher." TJ threw his empty beer bottle behind a tree and started up the trail.

Christopher and Johnny followed, carefully stepping around or over the rocks in the pathway. Christopher concentrated on stepping and breathing, stepping and breathing. The air was getting thinner, or was that his imagination? He hadn't felt so out of shape since he started fencing lessons with Johnny.

Johnny didn't seem bothered by the climb at all. At one point, he passed TJ and ran up to the next overlook.

"Geez, Johnny. You're not even out of breath at all," said Christopher when he caught up to him.

"It's the fencing. Keeps me in shape," said Johnny. "You should get back to it."

"Vassar doesn't have a fencing team," Christopher pointed out.

"Doesn't mean we can't still train," Johnny countered. "I can see about using the gym if you want, or we can use the park."

"Yeah, sure, maybe next semester. I'll let you know." Christopher enjoyed fencing, but he had other interests now. He collapsed onto a flat rock and turned his face up to enjoy the warm sun.

"This is nice!" Christopher said, leaning back on his elbows.

"Uh, Chris, don't move," said TJ quietly. "There's a… there's a…snake on that rock with you."

Christopher froze. "A snake?" he asked. "What kind of snake?" He hated snakes of all kinds. And then he heard the rattle.

"I think it's a rattlesnake," TJ said.

"No kidding." Christopher tried to keep his panic from showing. He held very, very still. "Get it away from me. Now, please."

"I'm not going near that thing," TJ said, backing up.

The snake turned its head and watched Johnny as he flicked a hand in its direction. "Hey, little rattlesnake," Johnny said in a friendly tone, "time to move on now. Leave my friend alone."

"It's a big snake," said TJ. "It's not a little snake."

"You're not helping, TJ," said Christopher.

The snake hissed and turned its head so that it was looking right at Christopher. Its dark dragon-like eyes had long, narrow, slit-like pupils that seemed way too intelligent for a snake. The tail rattled.

Christopher closed his eyes. Help me, please! The urgent request echoed in his head. He didn't dare speak out loud. Christopher wasn't sure who he was asking to help him. Neither Johnny nor TJ seemed to be acting on his behalf and, in this moment and in this situation, he wasn't sure they would.

Christopher felt a raindrop on his cheek. At least, he hoped it was a raindrop and not a tear. He would be super embarrassed to be crying in front of Johnny and TJ. Yes! It was a raindrop—a lot of raindrops! A dark cloud had appeared right above them. The air was quickly becoming chillier. He shivered as the rain drenched him. He opened one eye and saw the snake slither off the side of the rock and into the grass near the far edge of the trail.

"Oh man, did you see that?" TJ exclaimed. "You are the luckiest man ever, Chris. That was awesome."

"Glad you think so," said Christopher. "Remind me to check for snakes the next time I want to sit on a rock."

Johnny had been quiet.

"You all right Johnny? Did the snake spook ya?" TJ asked laughing.

"No. I actually like snakes," said Johnny distractedly. "Weird that it started raining all of a sudden. And now, poof, no more rain."

He was right. The rain had disappeared as fast as it had come. The dark cloud was gone and the warm sun was out again. They would dry off as they climbed the last part of the trail if the sun stayed out.

"Well, I'm fine. The snake is gone. Let's keep going." Christopher was anxious to get away from this spot. We're almost at the top."

They started up the last section of the trail. It was now almost completely smooth rock instead of dirt and jagged rocks like the lower portions of the trail had been. TJ had fun slipping and sliding. Christopher and Johnny were a bit more cautious, climbing slowly until they reached the base of the tower.

"You guys head up the tower if you want. I'm going to stay here and have another drink," said TJ, getting another beer from the backpack and a joint from his pocket.

"Let's do it," said Johnny putting a foot on the first rung of the ladder leading up to the top. "We've come this far."

"Count me out," said Christopher. "I've had enough excitement for the day. You go ahead, though. I'll wait here with TJ and catch my breath."

"Suit yourself," said Johnny as he expertly climbed up the tower. He waved from the top. "Whoo hoo! The view is amazing!" he shouted down.

"Told you!" TJ hollered back.

It was easier hiking back down the mountain than it had been going up. They arrived back at the dorms exhausted but exhilarated.

"Almost better than sex, right Chris?" TJ teased. "Exercise and adrenaline rush without the mess."

"You're a jerk, TJ," Christopher said. He didn't mean it. He thought maybe TJ was right.

CHAPTER 22

"What are you doing this summer?" Johnny asked Christopher after his freshman year finals were over. Christopher was packing up his stuff and waiting for his mom and dad to come pick him up.

"I don't know yet," Christopher said, throwing the last of his socks into a laundry bag.

"What would you think about coming with me to Turkey to meet some of my other brothers?"

Christopher looked at him in surprise. "I knew you came from a large family, but you've never talked about any of your siblings—other than Michael, of course. Now you want me to meet them?"

"Sure. Why not? I could use the company, and I think you'll really like them."

"Turkey? They live in Turkey? That's like halfway around the world."

"One brother, Peter, is an archeologist. The other, Julian, is a medical doctor. They work in Bergama. One of our best friends lives there, so Peter and Julian decided to move close to him a few years ago and they love it."

"Will I meet this friend too?" Christopher asked.

"Doubtful. He's pretty busy. But meeting my brothers is just as good."

"Wow. I'd like to go, but I have to ask my parents. They would have to fund me."

"Already done," Johnny said. "They said you can go if you want to. They'll buy your plane ticket. You'll stay with me and my brothers, so there's no expense to you for hotels or meals."

"You asked them already?" Christopher was a bit annoyed. He felt that was presumptuous of Johnny, but, then again, that also meant he didn't have to persuade his parents. They were already willing.

"Of course," Johnny explained. "I didn't want to ask you first and get your hopes up if they were going to say no."

"Oh." That made sense. "When do we leave?"

"Next week. We'll be back in time for the fall semester."

"Sounds great. Thanks, Johnny. I can't believe I'm going to meet your family."

"Yep. It will be nice to get away from here to a less… monitored…place. And I think I need the assistance right now."

Christopher wasn't sure what Johnny meant by that, so he shrugged and picked up a box.

"Help me take my stuff downstairs," he said to Johnny.

There wasn't much. Just clothes, bedding, and a few textbooks he hadn't been able to resell. They got it all downstairs to the curb in one trip. His parents pulled up and they loaded everything in the car.

"See you soon, Johnny," Christopher said as the car pulled away.

"Can't wait," Johnny replied with a smile.

They flew from JFK airport to Izmir Adnan Menderes Airport in Turkey a week later. Christopher slept the whole way, waking only when they had to change planes in Frankfurt, so it didn't seem like a long trip at all. He opened his eyes when he felt the plane touch down. Yawning and stretching, he said, "Are we there yet?"

Johnny laughed. "Yeah, we're here."

Christopher pulled open the shade and looked out the window.

"Looks hot out there," he said. The air looked wavy and shimmered in the sunlight.

Johnny just shrugged and stood up to get their carry-on luggage from the overhead compartment. They stepped out into the aisle and waited to make their way to the exit.

Christopher was curious about Johnny's family. Johnny hadn't told him much, and he didn't seem to want to talk about it when Christopher asked questions on the way here. Was he embarrassed by them? He had assumed they were all deadbeats, like Johnny's dad, but if one was an archeologist and the other was a doctor, well, they were certainly not deadbeats. Johnny was more of a deadbeat than they were—he was still in college "figuring out stuff" from what Christopher could see. Johnny and Michael must be the youngest of the siblings for Johnny to get away with that for so long. Come to think about it, Christopher didn't really know what Michael did either. He felt a little bad that he had never asked. The next time he saw him, he would definitely show more interest in Michael's life. Now, though, now he was about to start a summer adventure with Johnny. He would only think about that.

Two men that were unmistakably Johnny's brothers were waiting for them outside the baggage claim area. Both were very tall and looked a bit like bodybuilders. They had the same curly blond hair although one had hair that fell nearly to his shoulders and the other one had hair that was cut shorter, just barely covering the top of his ears. The shorter-haired brother had a beard and looked very serious. The other was grinning and came over to shake Johnny's hand and pat him on the back.

"Nice to see you, Johnny. It's been a while. The mission keeping you busy?"

"Yeah." To Christopher's surprise, Johnny looked uncomfortable. "That's actually why I'm here, but I'll fill you in later."

"This the one?" asked the serious brother in a deep, bass voice that resonated with confidence and authority. He nodded toward Christopher.

"Yeah. I said I'd fill you in later." Johnny was not happy and it showed in his voice. To Christopher, he seemed… was indignant the word for it? Or perhaps exasperated. His older brother was definitely not happy either. He looked like he would prefer to be anywhere else but here, picking up his little brother and an outsider.

"Christopher, this is Julian, the archeologist," Johnny said pointing toward the smiling one. "And this is Peter, the MD." He nodded toward the bearded brother.

"Nice to meet you both," said Christopher. "It's very kind of you to let me tag along for the summer." He wasn't sure if he should shake their hands, give them a hug, kiss their cheeks, or what. This was definitely not New York anymore. What did Turkish people do when they met? He wanted to be polite and respectful.

"Oh, believe me, it's our pleasure," said Julian in his playful tenor voice, putting an arm around Christopher's shoulders. He grinned as if he was sharing a private joke with someone. It couldn't be with Johnny or Peter, though. Neither one of them was smiling. Curious, Christopher thought. Maybe digging up bones and artifacts all day made a person a bit nuts. He liked Julian, though. Already he felt the same sort of bond with him that he felt with Johnny and Michael—or at least used to feel with Michael.

"Let's go," said Peter. "The car's parked out front."

They took their luggage and headed out the double doors. They drove north for about an hour and a half before arriving at Peter's villa in Bergama. It was a beautiful house, with three stories and a rooftop patio overlooking the city. Christopher's bedroom was on the third floor with easy access to the roof and he knew he would probably be spending a lot of time up there. It was cooler. He couldn't believe Peter's house wasn't air-conditioned. Peter and Julian seemed to have adapted to the heat and just stared at him when he asked about AC. This would definitely take some getting used to. It had to be like 120 degrees in the shade!

Christopher lay down on the bed. He was tired from the long trip, even though he had slept most of the way. Jet lag, he supposed. Johnny had suggested a nap and Christopher had eagerly agreed. As he lay on the bed, he heard the three brothers laughing and talking downstairs. He could only make out a few words as he drifted off to sleep: "mission"… "interference"…"help"… "the last one"… "can't fail"…

CHAPTER 23

The next morning, Peter, Julian, Johnny, and Christopher took the cable car to the top of the mountain. Passing by the vendors selling to tourists, they walked up the pathway to the ruins of an ancient city.

"This is where our family lives...lived," said Peter.

"A very long time ago," added Julian, "when it was called Pergamum." He led them through the main tourist areas, pointing out the remains of the city's theater, the passageway into the healing rooms, the stadium, the temples, and the shops. Christopher was amazed at how civilized it all seemed for such an ancient place.

Peter and Johnny didn't have much to say. They let Julian the archeologist do most of the talking. Peter added a few facts here and there when they were walking through the Asclepion. The medical history in this area was obviously more interesting to him. He told Christopher that the gods had sent messages in dreams to the physicians so they would know how to heal the people that came to the school of medicine associated with the temple of Asklepios. Snakes were very prominent in the symbols used for the medical center. They were also at one time used in the rituals—non-venomous ones of course, Peter clarified. Yikes!

To be truthful, Christopher was a little bored with the tour and a little creeped out by the snakes. It was too soon after the hiking incident for him to feel any affection at all for snakes. And he had never liked history. Ruins were just rocks and columns that had fallen over. The only part that was even a little interesting was that this was where Johnny's family was from.

"You know, Johnny, I never knew your family was from Turkey. You don't look Turkish," Christopher noticed.

"Ah, well, there's a lot you don't know, isn't there?" Johnny teased.

"Tell me about your father," Christopher said. "Is he here in Turkey too? Can I meet him? Where are the rest of your siblings? Don't you have like 15 of them?" he exaggerated.

"I have so many siblings I can't keep track." Johnny was telling the truth for once, but Christopher gave him a playful push.

"Stop with the evasiveness! I don't know why you are so embarrassed to tell me," Christopher complained. "Growing up, you made it sound like they are all terrible deadbeats and your dad kicked you all out, but Peter and Julian are very successful. I really like them. Did your father really kick you out when you were younger? Or did you just run away or something?"

"Deadbeats? He called us deadbeats?" Julian had overheard their conversation. "Well, my, my! What a nice thing to say, brother." Julian was laughing. "Speak for yourself!"

"He...he...didn't exactly call you...deadbeats. That's just what I assumed because he...never talked about you at all," Christopher stammered. Oh boy. He was making this worse.

Julian raised an eyebrow. "Oh really? Never? Well, we don't talk about him much either," he joked.

"You won't meet our father. He doesn't like it here," said Peter. "You might meet more of our siblings, though. Time will tell."

That sounded mysterious, Christopher thought. Oh well, if they didn't want to talk about their family, he would let it drop—for now.

"Let's go to the top," suggested Johnny. "You can see the whole city from there."

The brothers started up the rocky path. Christopher had no choice but to join them. He fell behind—they were much more athletic than he was! To be fair, he was not used to rock climbing or this heat and they were. A few more days of this and he was sure he would be in just as great a shape as they were. After a few minutes, they were so far ahead that Christopher decided to sit down and rest. It was really hot! They didn't even notice he wasn't with them anyway. It looked like they were very deep in a serious conversation.

"I've tried but someone keeps getting in the way." Christopher recognized Johnny's voice. "It's not Michael. I could take care of that. It's other things, like his friends, or the weather, or..."

"We just have to keep him from believing. It's not that hard." Peter's voice was unmistakable.

"Until he dies," said Julian cheerfully. "Then we have foiled the plan and it's done! Success!"

Christopher hoped they were not talking about him. It must be the heat making him delusional. He took a long drink of water and closed his eyes. He could still hear the voices but not the words. He would wait here until they came back.

"I think I've got him to the point where he's so deep in sexual activity and alcohol that he'll believe he's not good enough if the invitation to meet our father ever comes up." Johnny said.

"Drugs? Have you gotten him into drugs? That's a sure thing," Julian suggested.

"I tried," Johnny said defensively.

"You tried?" mocked Peter. "You are supposed to be the best of us and you only tried?" His eyes narrowed into snake-like slits and his voice became threatening. "I wanted this assignment. I could have gotten the job done by now."

"Well, you weren't given the assignment. I was. And I will get the job done. This is my plan and it's brilliant." Johnny was even more defensive and angry now. "I thought my brothers could help, might even want to help, but no thanks, I'll do it myself." He started to turn away but Julian held his arm in a vise-like grip.

"We are going to help, Johnny," he said. "You need us. You know you need us. That's why you came." He looked almost reptilian standing in the shadow of the only tree this high up the mountain and his voice was ugly, not laughing or cheerful anymore.

"Let's just push him off this cliff," Peter said.

"Wait, where is he?" asked Julian.

"Safe and sound on the rock ledge below," replied Johnny. "And you know we can't physically harm him ourselves so ix-nay on the pushing. He has to do it or another person has to do it, or it has to be an accident, etc, etc. We have been forbidden to hurt him."

"Hmmpf," growled Peter. "That makes it a little more difficult, doesn't it?"

"As I said..." Johnny was trying to be patient with these fools. He really did need them. This mission was harder than he had thought it would be.

"Let's go get Christopher and head home. I have an idea," said Julian. He prided himself on being a master manipulator and was confident he could best Johnny in this little competition to corrupt the boy.

When they got back to the villa, Julian suggested the four of them go sit on the rooftop to cool off. He brought up four cups of Turkish tea and four bottles of water, and put them down on a small table before sitting down on a chair near Christopher.

"What is that?" Christopher asked, pointing to a hookah sitting prominently on a low table near their chairs.

"It's called Mu'assel or hookah." Julian said, delighted that Christopher had asked. "We use it to relax on a hot afternoon. This one has been in our family for centuries. Here, let me show you how it works."

He attached a silicon hose to the stem and dropped coconut coals in a charcoal burner. While they were heating up, Julian carefully measured out some water and poured it into the beautiful glass bowl base that Christopher had noticed. He set the stem inside the glass bowl. Next, he put what looked to Christopher like berry-red sticky tobacco leaves into a small clay bowl shaped like an hourglass and lightly packed it down into the larger end. He added foil to the top to cover it then poked holes in the foil all the way around. He attached the base on top of the stem, and set the clay bowl on top of that and the now-white coals on top of that. It was quite a process. Christopher was fascinated.

When it had heated up to just the right temperature, Julian put the hose in his mouth and pulled in the smoke in a long breath. He slowly blew out the smoke and sighed with happiness. Peter reached for the hose and took a turn. Johnny was next. As he blew out the smoke, he handed the hose to Christopher.

"This is really good," Johnny told Christopher. "I missed this. It's been a while since I've enjoyed a good hookah."

Christopher held the hose and just looked at it. "It's like smoking. I don't smoke. Well, except for that one cigar…"

"Nah," said Julian. "It doesn't taste anything like smoking. Just try it. You put the hose in your mouth and pull with a deep breath. If you don't like it, you don't have to do it."

"We wouldn't do it if it was not healthy," added Peter.

Christopher thought for a minute. If the doctor said it was OK, then it must be. Besides, they had done this for generations. They all looked like body builders and were in great physical shape so… Christopher put the hose in his mouth and pulled in the smoke. He felt light-headed, but the taste was really good. He blew out the smoke slowly like he had seen them do. He didn't even cough. He liked this better than the cigar.

"Have another," encouraged Julian.

Christopher did.

They passed around the hookah hose until there was no more, then lay back in their chairs and watched the sunset. Life could not get better than this, thought Christopher. This was perfect. This was Heaven.

CHAPTER 24

They went dancing, enjoyed the hookah almost every night, leered at pretty women, drank raki, and slept late. Christopher briefly wondered how Peter and Julian could take so much time off of work, but he figured they had lots of vacation stored up and were using it to make sure he and Johnny had a good time. He didn't give it a second thought.

Christopher's brain felt a little foggier every day. He couldn't always remember what he had done the day before, or the day before that. However, his wit must be sharper than ever—obviously—since the three brothers laughed at almost everything he said or did. They dared him to do stuff, like balance on the rooftop ledge or eat fish eyes or "accidentally" touch a passing woman's butt, then laughed hysterically when he did whatever the dare of the day was. Christopher enjoyed the attention and the freedom to do whatever he pleased. The three months passed quickly.

The night before he and Johnny were supposed to fly home, as they were enjoying their last meal together, Christopher told the brothers he wished he could just stay there with them and never go back to the United States or to school. He would like the rest of his life to be this fun.

The brothers stole triumphal glances at each other and told Christopher he was welcome to stay as long as he liked.

"Great!" Christopher was elated. "I'll call my parents and..."

"No!" The three brothers shouted at the same time.

"Uh...you're almost 20! Do you really have to get permission?" asked Julian as Christopher ran out of the room to make the phone call.

"Too late," said Peter.

"You see? Something or someone always interferes just when I think I have him." Johnny was seething. "You know they are going to say no."

"My parents said no," said Christopher coming back into the room, frowning. "They want me to finish college. But," he continued, "they said I could come back every summer if I want to. I didn't tell them this, but I think I will look for a job here after I graduate. Not archeology or medicine, but there's gotta be something I can do here, right? I wanna stay with you guys forever. This has been so much fun!"

The three nodded mutely.

"Guess I'd better go pack then," said Christopher, running upstairs and leaving the three of them sitting there, none of them knowing what to say.

"Me too, I guess." Johnny broke the silence. "Thanks for your help," he said to his brothers sarcastically. "This was an overwhelming success. I don't know what I will do without you."

"Shut up," growled Peter. "We kept him distracted all summer and away from anything that could influence him the other way. You should be grateful."

"Well, I'm not."

"You're on your own then. Keep us out of it. I don't want my name mentioned when you are punished for your ineptitude. You'll be thrown in the pit and good riddance to you." Peter was determined not to take any blame.

Julian looked delighted. There was nothing better than a good fight. He flexed his fingers, wishing he could let the claws loose. Oh, to be in his own skin again! One more day. Just one more day...

Johnny caught a glimpse of the scales rippling on the back of Peter's neck and saw his eyes narrow into tiny slits as anger won out over his self-control. His face contorted into snarling reptile-like features for a brief moment and he reached out toward Johnny's throat with six knobby, sharp claws on each hand.

"Stop!" Johnny commanded. Peter obeyed. He had no choice. Johnny was in charge of this mission. He quickly relaxed back into human form with a handsome human face and hands.

Johnny turned and looked with disdain at Julian and Peter. "I'm done with you. You can both go to Hell." He turned and walked away. Peter snarled and Julian laughed as they, too, walked out the door into the darkness.

CHAPTER 25

Johnny was uncharacteristically quiet on the flight home. He sat by the window, just staring out at the clouds and drinking Scotch. He had to think. He was usually very good at his job, taking the number one spot time after time. He had been so good that the big boss had taken notice and assigned him this mission specifically. He could not fail. He would just have to think of something. There was always a key—always a solution.

Christopher watched movies and slept a little, so he didn't really notice anything out of the ordinary with his friend until they were on the last leg of their journey.

"What's up?" Christopher asked Johnny. "You're awfully quiet. Missing your family already?"

"Not at all. We had a bit of a fight last night, so I am actually glad to be headed back. Too much of a good thing, ya know?" Johnny took a sip of his Scotch.

"Well, I liked them a lot. They were super fun. Just like you!" Christopher said. "Except for now. You're not fun right now."

"Sorry buddy. I'm just doing a lot of thinking and I'm frustrated...I mean tired. I'm tired. Long trip and all..."

"I was just kidding, Johnny." Christopher frowned. "You know I was just kidding, right?"

"Sure." Johnny turned his face back toward the window. "We'll be landing in a couple of hours. Why don't you watch another movie to pass the time?"

Christopher shrugged and put his headphones back on. He flipped through the choices and selected an action movie he hadn't seen in a while. He settled back into the seat and decided to just ignore Johnny until he cheered up. This black mood he was in was not something Christopher wanted any part of. He was still flying high from the great time he had had in Turkey and wanted to hang on to that feeling as long as he could.

They landed without incident, sailed through customs, and headed to the baggage claim area. Teresa and Joseph were there to meet them and gave each one a long hug and a kiss on both cheeks.

"We missed you so much!" said Teresa. "I'm making your favorite meal for dinner tonight and I invited your friends to join us. Let's go!"

Joseph picked up a suitcase in each hand and led them out of the airport to the passenger pickup area where a limo was waiting for them. Christopher got in the car, but Johnny hung back.

"I'm going to meet someone here in the city for dinner. I'll catch up with you later," Johnny told them.

"Are you sure?" Teresa asked him. "I've got cannolis for dessert!"

"I'm sure. See you!"

"OK. Thanks for everything, Johnny. Thanks for bringing Christopher back safely," Teresa said as she and Joseph joined Christopher in the car.

"Mom, what did you mean about friends joining us? Which friends? From college?" Christopher asked apprehensively as the car pulled away from the curb and out into traffic. His mother did not really know who his friends were anymore. She knew his roommate, but his other friends—probably not.

"No, honey. From here. From your hometown. There's Tony and Crystal and Jack's boy Domenic."

"I don't know a Domenic."

"Sure you do. He was in your confirmation class. He's your second cousin, I think."

"And I haven't spoken to Tony and Crystal in like a year."

"It'll be fun. Don't you worry," Teresa said, patting his cheek. She chatted on about the rest of the family—which cousin was getting married, who was having a baby, who was getting out of jail—things he didn't really care about, but he did enjoy hearing his mom's voice. It had been three months! He hadn't realized until now how much he had missed his family.

"Tell us about the trip, Christopher," his father said. "We want to hear all about Johnny's brothers and how they kept you busy. I hope you were respectful. I've taught you to always be respectful."

"Julian was funny. He is the archeologist. We went to some ruins and he tried to teach me stuff, but you know how I am with history. It was kinda cool but a total loss for me learning anything." Christopher laughed at himself. "And Peter is a doctor and sorta tough on the outside, but he was cool too. I saw where his ancestors practiced medicine. They used snakes. Uggh!" He shivered involuntarily.

Christopher didn't want to tell his parents what they really did in Turkey. He knew they would not approve and would probably never let him go back if he told them everything, so he just skipped over the good parts and told them the boring stuff. His mother clucked approvingly, and his father nodded and asked the driver how much longer it would be until they got home. It was late and he was hungry.

It wasn't long. Tony came running over to the car as they pulled up in front of the house and helped Christopher carry his suitcases up the steps and into his bedroom.

"Hey, man. Welcome home. I didn't even know you were out of the country until your mom called me this week. That's so cool. So cool."

"Yeah. It was a lot of fun." Christopher was less than enthusiastic to see Tony. "Where's Crystal?" He was a little more enthusiastic to see her.

"She'll be here soon. She wanted to pick up balloons or something. Girls are so sentimental." Tony thought he was being funny. Christopher thought he was just a dweeb.

"You'll never guess what happened to me, Chris. I can't wait to tell you."

"What?" Christopher knew he sounded bored but he couldn't help it. He was bored.

"I became a Christian."

Christopher rolled his eyes. "All good Italians are Christian. You can't become one. You just are."

"No, no, that's not right, man. You have to decide to follow Jesus Christ. Get it? That's where the name Christian comes from—follower of Christ."

"Yeah, whatever," Christopher said under his breath. He didn't really want to hear about Tony.

Crystal knocked on the bedroom door.

"Hi guys," she said, smiling. "Are you talking about me?"

"Come on in—please!" said Christopher. "Rescue me from this crazy guy here who tells me he is now a Jesus freak." He was surprised at how happy he was to see Crystal. His heart did a little flip as she walked into his room.

"What makes you think he is a freak?" she asked.

"He's talking about following Jesus—who is dead, by the way. Hanging on a cross, so unless he means that he too has a death wish, I don't see how that is possible," Christopher joked.

"You know Jesus didn't stay dead, right?" Crystal asked. "He was killed on the cross and buried, but He came back to life after three days."

"That's insane. Nobody comes back to life after three days. After a few minutes, sure, I've heard those stories, but three days? No way." Christopher couldn't believe Crystal had bought into this.

"You're right," she said and Christopher breathed a sigh of relief.

"But…" she continued, "Jesus wasn't a normal person. He was God—is God. There was no other way to fix what humans had ruined so He came Himself as a man to fix it. In order to do that, He had to die so He could defeat death and save us."

"Crystal, you are not making sense." Christopher told her.

"Sorry if this is a little confusing. Maybe I'm not explaining it well but it is real to me. All I know is that I don't deserve to go to Heaven because it's perfect there and I am not perfect. Jesus wants me to be there with Him so He came to earth to take the punishment that should have been mine."

"It's like Jack," interjected Tony. "You know how he wanted to be at his daughter's wedding but he almost couldn't be there because he did that thing—you know, that thing that should have sent him to prison for life?"

"Yeah," said Christopher.

"But Jerry went to the cops and said it was his fault and he would do the time because he loved Jack like a brother and didn't want him to miss his daughter's wedding?"

"Yeah," repeated Christopher.

"It's like that with Jesus. We deserve the punishment but Jesus wants us to be in Heaven with Him so He accepted a death penalty to pay for our crimes—the church calls them "sins"—even though He didn't do anything wrong. That satisfied the Judge, who is God by the way, and we get to go free. And the cool thing is that He didn't stay dead. Ha! The joke was on the devil who tried to keep Him dead. Because Jesus is God, He fought through death and came out on the other side—alive! It's crazy, man!" Christopher had never seen Tony so excited about anything. He really believed this stuff.

"It sure is crazy, Tony. I don't know what to say," Christopher told him.

"We want you to meet the Father too," said Crystal.

"The Father?" asked Christopher, startled. This was starting to sound a bit like conversations he had had with Michael and Johnny about their family.

"God," said Tony.

"Oh yeah, I remember. God the Father, Jesus the Son, and the Holy Spirit. Three in one," Christopher said. "More magic mumbo jumbo."

Crystal sighed. "You'll understand it when you're ready."

"Kids, time for dinner!" Teresa shouted from the kitchen. "Wash up and come to the table!"

Christopher led the way to the dining room, and they all sat around the table piled high with more food than they could possibly eat in one sitting.

"You've been busy, Mom," Christopher remarked.

"Well, I've missed you," she said. "So eat up. There's more in the kitchen. Eat! Eat!"

They passed around the food. Christopher noticed that Tony and Crystal bowed their heads and closed their eyes for about 30 seconds before they ate anything. Neither said a word, but Christopher knew they were praying. Sometimes his family did that when the priest came to dinner but it was usually out loud. He wondered what they were saying to God inside their heads. What did they need to keep so secret? Was it about him? This was going to drive him crazy until he knew but he couldn't ask with his mom and dad right there. That conversation would have to wait.

"Can Christopher come with us to Bible study tomorrow?" asked Crystal sweetly.

"Bible what?" said Joseph.

Tony glanced gratefully at Crystal. "What a good idea," he said. "Bible study. It's at the college."

"And it's free," added Crystal.

"Oh, a college class. Of course," said Joseph. "Good to get back into the swing of things before the semester starts."

"It will help things make more sense," Crystal told Christopher. "You know, the things we were talking about before."

Christopher found he couldn't resist her. That old attraction was still there so he shrugged and said, "Sure. I'll go."

"Great!" Crystal said, smiling at Christopher with her big brown eyes. "That's terrific! You'll love it."

CHAPTER 26

Christopher wasn't sure he'd love Bible study, but he drove over to pick up Tony and then Crystal the next evening after dinner. He did love driving his Mustang again. He guessed that was about the only thing he would miss when he moved to Turkey in a few years.

To his relief, Crystal and Tony said nothing about Jesus on the drive to the college. He parked the Mustang in the middle of two spots so that no one would open a car door and scratch it. He always took precautions, knowing that other students weren't as proud or as careful with their cars as he was. Nothing was going to happen to this baby!

Christopher followed Tony and Crystal into one of the Terrace Apartments on the Vassar College campus. Several students had already gathered in the common area. Christopher didn't recognize any of them. This was not his usual crowd. They were drinking soda and snacking on raw vegetables. He took a soda but skipped the veggies. Yuck.

Crystal introduced him to the group. What were their names again? Steve and Cathy and Eric? He didn't know why he bothered to try to remember since he probably would not be coming again. A man named Terry seemed to be the leader. He shook Christopher's hand and indicated that he should sit in one of the big armchairs.

Everyone else took a seat on the couch or the floor. Terry sat in the other armchair and opened a Bible. The other students had Bibles too. Christopher thought that he probably looked like a dork sitting there with nothing. Crystal smiled and handed him an extra Bible she had brought with her. OK, he was feeling better now. Leave it to Crystal to make him feel comfortable in this very weird setting with people he didn't know.

Terry asked them all to turn to Acts 1:11 and read something about Jesus coming back from Heaven in the clouds. It couldn't be any more weird. Would He be coming in a space ship or something? Christopher wondered what Father Giovanni or that young priest would think of that idea.

"For some reason, I feel God wants us to look at the book of I Thessalonians tonight." Terry flipped the pages of his Bible. "It's near the end of the book. Can someone read I Thessalonians 4?"

The girl named Cathy raised her hand. "I have it!"

Christopher listened politely as she began reading. He almost choked on his soda when she read, "It is God's will that you should be sanctified: that you should avoid sexual immorality…" and then—holy cow—"the Lord will punish all those who commit such sins…" Well, he was definitely going to be punished then because he was not giving up sex. Jesus freaks and celibates. Definitely not his crowd. Christopher checked his watch. It had only been ten minutes.

Cathy kept droning on, but two words caught Christopher's attention. Death. Hope. This passage was talking about death and hope in the same sentence. There was no hope in death. Death was death. Death was the end. Everything over. Nothing more. Where was the hope in that? And what was this about the Lord shouting and trumpets playing and angels—for Pete's sake, really? Angels? And getting taken up in the sky to meet God?

Nope. This was definitely not for him. Why did people think they needed God anyway? Christopher believed this was just something people had invented to either guilt people into doing what they wanted or to force people to give up their money to other people who pretended to be better than anyone else.

Christopher didn't listen much to the rest of the lesson. Terry tried to pull him into the discussion, but he just shrugged or said, "I don't know" to every question. Crystal was frowning and Tony kept looking at him as if he was the idiot.

These people wanted him to give up sex and probably everything else that was fun—for what? To go to a mythical place when he died? No way. He was going to enjoy life and then whatever happened after that, happened. He was pretty sure the whatever was nothing.

"I've got to go soon," Christopher told Tony when Terry wrapped up the discussion.

"You go ahead, Chris," Tony told him. "Crystal and I can get a ride from Cathy. She lives over near me."

"Suit yourself," said Christopher. He left without saying goodbye to any of them and didn't see them gather in a circle, holding hands, praying for him.

Christopher got in his car and slammed the door. Why had he ever agreed to go? It was hard to believe that modern-day people still believed in God. Humans had evolved over millions of years to become smarter than that. And this Jesus stuff? Christopher believed there had been a man named Jesus a few thousand years ago but he didn't understand all the fuss over Him. There was no way He had magically come alive after being dead three days. That was a story people had invented to control other people by saying the only way to Heaven was through Jesus and the only way to Jesus was through the church. And, of course, you had to pay for all the services the church provided. It was all about control and money, money and control.

Christopher shook his head in disgust as he put the car in gear, turned on his headlights, drove across the college campus, and pulled out onto Raymond Avenue. There was no one in the traffic circle so he blew through that and headed toward the Arterial. The light at the corner turned yellow but Christopher didn't see anyone coming so he pulled out, starting to make a left turn into the westbound lane.

Turning his head once more to check, Christopher saw a pickup truck appear out of nowhere, coming fast in the same lane. Before he could make the turn, the truck hit him,

T-boning him on the passenger side. His head slammed against the window, and his vision quickly began to narrow from wide angle to tunnel and then turned completely to black. His car was pushed across the road and came to a stop on top of metal poles that had, until a split second ago, been holding up a one-way sign. Steam escaped from under the hood as witnesses raced over to see if the driver of the crumpled, apple-red 1969 Mustang was okay.

Christopher thought he was just fine. He stood just behind his car and watched as the flashing lights of an ambulance, firetruck, and police cars came rushing to the scene. The firemen were using some sort of tool to pry the door of the car off. Well, that was strange. He was right here. Who were they trying to rescue?

A bright light flashed on his left. Another one flashed on his right. Two vaporous giants appeared about twenty feet in front of him. They held very, very large swords, which they were swinging at each other using masterful strokes intended to kill. This was not a game. Sparks went flying as the swords hit again and again. Wait! That looked like Michael with the first sword and he was fighting…Johnny?

Both of the beings had large wings protruding out of their backs that spread about six feet on either side of their bodies. The first one radiated light like the sun. The other sucked light in like a black hole.

"He's mine," the dark one that looked like Johnny growled. "I'm taking him. It's over. He's dead. You lose."

"No. I claim him for the Father. You cannot have him," the bright one that looked like Michael said very loudly.

Christopher rubbed his eyes. What the heck? Were these aliens? Or angels? Or maybe they were the same thing—angels were aliens and aliens were angels? He was so confused. Why were they fighting? Weren't angels just supposed to play harps and pass along messages?

The swords swished and clanged as the two beings skillfully parried. Christopher heard whistling sounds as the swords cut through the air and attempted to hit their targets. There were sparks flying everywhere. He couldn't help but admire their technique. Those were some of the moves he had learned from Johnny! He ducked as the one who looked like Johnny swung a sword over his head in a large circle before thrusting it forward toward the other being. He missed.

"Christopher will live," said the one that looked like Michael, dodging the blow. "You cannot touch him."

"Says who?" crowed the Johnny lookalike, hitting his target in the shoulder with the side of his blade. The first being winced but kept fighting.

This is surreal, thought Christopher. He glanced away from the two fighters and saw the firemen pull his body out of the car and lay him on the ground. Was he dead? Was this the "whatever" that came after death? He started to panic. He needed to get out of here, but his legs were not responding. He couldn't move. He tried to tug at his legs but his hands went right through them. He had no…what was the word? He had no substance. He was like the air itself. Now he really started to panic!

The Johnny alien grew bigger and uglier and more intimidating. Johnny's face became gruesome—twisted where faces don't normally twist with black and purple streaks around reptilian eyes. He gripped the sword with superhuman strength. His long, pointed claws, poison dripping from each of the twelve razor sharp digits, were ready to scratch his opponent in close combat if the sword failed. Christopher had never been so frightened in all of his life. He felt a dark evil radiating from the ugly one and tried to back up, but the evil held him there. It gripped him tightly around the ankles and would not let him go.

Christopher heard faint voices. They sounded like the voices of the people he had just left at the college. Were they... praying? He couldn't understand the words, but the bright angel seemed to be drawing strength from it. He seemed to grow bigger and brighter and more powerful with every word. The ugly one covered the holes on the side of his head that were his ears and screamed obscenities.

"Go!" commanded the bright one. The ugly one snarled, growled, shrieked, and tried to resist, but the bright one thrust his sword through the chest of the ugly one and he disappeared in a puff of smoke.

It was suddenly quiet. Christopher looked over at the car and saw paramedics performing CPR—on him? He looked up at the bright one and felt... and felt... peace, joy, warmth, love...and emotions he didn't even know how to express.

"Who are you?" Christopher asked. "Am I dead?"

"Christopher, it's me—Michael. And, no, you are not dead."

"Michael? You're an angel or something? How could I not know that? You've been around me my whole life. And who was that other guy?" Christopher shuddered. "He looked an awful lot like Johnny."

"That was the being you know as Johnny. Although he was an angel once, he made his choice to reject God and join forces with Satan. He is a demon. A very powerful demon."

"No way. Johnny was good, and fun. I just spent the whole summer with him. We…" Christopher stopped, realizing the truth. "I guess we didn't always do what was good."

"I was sent by God to protect you and he was sent by Satan to destroy you," Michael explained. "He used that fun stuff to try to win you over as well as to distract you and destroy your life. Fortunately, he wasn't always as successful as he hoped he'd be."

Christopher shuddered again. He had been terrified by the Johnny he had just seen. "I'm sure glad you won this fight—you did win didn't you? Johnny won't be back?"

"I don't know. I think his time is over, but that's up to the Father." said Michael.

"OK. Good." Christopher thought for a minute. "Why do you call God father? All this time when you talked about your father, you meant God?"

"Yes. God created angels so He is our father in that way."

"Johnny's father too? He said his father kicked him out."

"Yes, God created Johnny too—and Satan. But when Satan decided he wanted to be a god even more powerful than the Father, he persuaded many of the other angels to join him and there was a battle. Of course, God won and Satan and his angels had to leave Heaven. They were sent here, to earth, and have been trying to undermine God ever since. Every human they can prevent from having a relationship with God makes their army stronger. From Adam until now it has been their number one goal to redo that fight with God and win it. They don't want you—or any human—to know God, to love Him, or to have a relationship with Him. They want you for their army, not His. What they don't want to believe is that God doesn't need humans to make his army strong. God is strong enough all by Himself. God wants humans—to talk with Him, to love Him, and to live with Him. And that's all. Satan will use you and abuse you for his own purposes. God loves you just because you are you. Satan lies and takes. God loves and gives."

"I don't get it. Why would God care about me? Does everyone have angels fighting over them? And why didn't you guys ever tell me about this?" Christopher really, really wanted to know.

"God has a plan for everything and his timing is perfect. I couldn't tell you until He allowed me to. He wants you to know now."

"But why now? I've done some bad things, although I've mostly been good..." Christopher felt guilty. "If God loves everyone, why doesn't He just make everybody love Him?

Why hide away up in Heaven? Why doesn't He just show Himself if He wants me to know Him? Why make me wreck my car and go through this?" He pointed to the paramedics loading his body into the ambulance.

"You have a lot of good questions that would take more time than we have right now to answer. But, I can tell you that perhaps you will appreciate Him more because you recognize that you can't live your life the way you want to without messing it up somewhere along the way. His way is always better, but He won't force you to accept that. He loved you enough to let you decide for yourself."

"Not everyone gets this deathbed chance, do they?" Christopher asked.

"No," said Michael sadly.

"Why me? What's so special about me?"

"You're the last one," said Michael.

"What do you mean, the last one?" Christopher was puzzled.

"The last human to choose life or death before Jesus can return to earth to take His people home."

"Is that home? Is that Heaven?" asked Christopher, pointing to the twinkling space behind Michael. He didn't understand the "return to earth" part, but he had heard about Heaven.

"Yes, that's the door," Michael replied. "You are feeling the presence of God just beyond it —His love, joy, peace…"

"I do feel that. It's awesome! Let's go," said Christopher. "I want to go to Heaven where God is! Please, please take me there!" he begged. "I don't want to go back."

But Christopher felt his body tugging at him as he spoke, pulling him back from this in-between space. As he took a deep breath, Michael faded out of view, but not before Christopher heard him say, "Jesus is the way. Find Jesus."

CHAPTER 27

Christopher woke up in the hospital, disoriented and bruised. His whole body was sore and he could see that his left leg was in a cast. The beeping of a monitor just out of his sight was perfectly in sync with the thumping in his head. He felt awful.

A nurse came over to take his pulse and blood pressure. "Nice to see that you're awake," she said, smiling. "You've been out for two days."

"Tagle dura?" Christopher had meant to say, "two days?" but it came out all jumbled.

The nurse laughed kindly and said, "You'll be fine. Just rest. You had some internal injuries, a broken leg, and a very bad concussion, but the doctors have taken care of it all. Your job now is just to rest and let your body heal itself. You'll be in ICU for a few more days. I'm putting morphine in your IV to help you sleep."

"Flaggle," said Christopher. That means thanks, he thought. I hope you know that means thanks. He drifted off to sleep.

It was actually five more days before Christopher was released from the ICU and settled in a private hospital room.

His mother and father had insisted on a private room and D'Antonis always got their way. His mother hardly ever left his side and his father came right after work to sit with him every evening. When he started to feel better, his father brought cards so they could play. Christopher tired easily and couldn't always tell a king from a jack, but he tried not to let on. He didn't want his parents to worry.

He worried, though. He worried a lot. Sometimes the words didn't come out the way he wanted them to. There were things he couldn't remember. There were things he did remember but wasn't sure they were true. Had he hallucinated? The nurse said sometimes that happened with a traumatic brain injury. He wasn't going to mention those memories to anyone, though, because he was worried they would classify him as a mental patient and lock him up in a hospital forever. He just wanted out of here. He wanted to get back to normal. He had missed the fall semester because of the accident, but should be good to go by the spring semester. He hoped.

Crystal knocked on his hospital room door. "Hi Mr. and Mrs. D'Antoni. How's Chris doing?"

His mom looked up from her knitting. "Hello, dear. It was nice of you to come. He's doing fine. Right, Christopher? You're doing fine?" Teresa patted Christopher's hand and put her knitting aside.

"Come on in, Crystal," said Joseph. "I'm sure Christopher would love to see you."

Christopher nodded and waved. He didn't trust his words completely yet.

Crystal came in the room and set a vase of flowers on the windowsill. "You look okay," she told Christopher. "Apart from the Frankenstein stitches on your shaved head and the bruises under your eyes. Just being real," she added with a smile when she saw the shocked look on his face as he reached up to touch the left side of his head.

Teresa laughed nervously. "He's as handsome as ever. Don't worry, Christopher. Everything will heal in time."

Joseph cleared his throat. "Uh, Teresa, let's go get some dinner and let Crystal and Christopher have some time alone."

"Oh!" Teresa was surprised that Christopher might not want his mother there, but she recovered quickly. "Of course. Let's go to the cafeteria. The food there is not too bad. We'll be back soon, Christopher."

"OK, Ma," he said.

Joseph guided Teresa out of the room and Crystal sat in the chair next to the bed.

"So how are you really doing?" she asked.

"I'm getting better," Christopher said evasively.

"We were praying for you—the Bible study group, I mean—when the accident happened. It's the weirdest thing, but we all had this feeling that you needed us to pray for you and, well, you did, but we didn't find out that you did until the next day."

"You were praying for me?"

"Yes."

"I thought I heard you."

"Really? You left so quickly I didn't think you even noticed."

"No, I mean, I didn't hear you when I left. I heard you after the accident." Now why had he told her that? Shut up, Christopher, he told himself.

"So you had a weird experience, too?" Crystal didn't seem surprised. "Tell me about it."

Christopher wasn't sure he could trust her, but she took his hand in hers and looked in his eyes with her big brown ones. "Whatever you say, I believe you. You can tell me."

Instead of telling her, Christopher asked, "Have you seen Johnny lately? Or Michael?"

"No," she said. "Your mom said Johnny had gone back to Turkey. She tried to call him after the accident, but it went to voicemail. The message was, 'Hi, this is Johnny. I'll be in Turkey for a while and may not be able to pick up my voicemail. Catch you later!' That was it."

"What about Michael? Have you seen him?"

"No, come to think about it. We haven't seen him either. I think your mom talked to him on the phone, though. He said he is praying for you, too. Well, actually his exact words were, 'Let Christopher know I will be at home talking to the Father about him.' We sometimes say 'talking to the Father' when we're referring to prayer," she explained. Crystal didn't know how much Christopher understood about prayer and God.

"Oh," said Christopher. He looked upset.

"What does 'the last one' mean?" he asked her. "Is that a Bible thing?"

Crystal furrowed her brow, thinking hard. "I don't think I've ever heard of that phrase. Why do you ask?"

"I mean, is there something in the Bible about God suddenly taking His people home, to Heaven?"

"Oh! You mean the rapture. Sure. You know that after Jesus rose from the dead, He met with his disciples and crowds of believers so they would know it was really Him. Then, while some of His disciples watched, He was lifted up into the clouds and went back to Heaven. He told them He would come back someday, in just the same way. When He does, all of the believers will be taken up into the clouds with Him. Those lucky enough to be here for that won't die. They will just be changed from this physical body that we have now to a new one and then enter Heaven. That's called the rapture."

Christopher was listening carefully. He didn't want to miss a word. If what she was saying didn't sound crazy to people—and obviously it didn't because thousands of people all over the world believed it—then maybe his story wouldn't sound crazy to Crystal either.

"What do you mean by believers?" he asked. Christopher wanted to make sure he got this right. "Not everyone will go?"

"No. I think very few will go. There are a lot of people who say they are Christians but they don't believe that Jesus died for their sins, rose again, and lives in Heaven, or that He is coming back for those who do believe—His people." Crystal put air quotes around "His people" as she spoke. "There's a difference between Christianity and actually believing in Jesus Christ. Christianity is a religion. Believing in Jesus is a relationship."

"I'm not religious. In fact, I d-d-despise religion. It's just people trying to c-c-c-ontrol other people." Christopher was adamant. He was embarrassed by his stutter, but also relieved that at least he got the right words out this time, not gibberish.

"You don't have to be religious to be a believer," Crystal said, ignoring the stutter. "In fact, believers come from all kinds of religions and churches, or no church at all. The one thing in common is that they have a personal one-on-one relationship with Jesus and have acknowledged Him as their Savior."

"What about those that believe in Mohammed? Or Buddha?"

"There's only one God and the way to Heaven—His home—is through Him. Don't you think He has the right to tell us how to get to His house? It's demonic spiritual beings who don't want you to get there and who try to distract you and lead you down roads that may circle Heaven but never actually get you there."

"That's kinda what Michael told me. I've been distracted by other pe...things."

"When did you talk to Michael?" Crystal asked him.

Christopher didn't answer right away. Crystal waited patiently and didn't speak.

"Well, I'll tell you but you have to promise not to laugh or run away screaming. And you can NOT tell my parents. They'll have me committed."

"This sounds interesting," said Crystal leaning back in the chair. "Do tell!"

"Promise me first."

"OK, OK, I promise!" Crystal's face was serious, giving Christopher the confidence to continue.

"When I had the accident, I was outside of my body for a few minutes and I saw things."

Crystal nodded. "The paramedics said your heart stopped and they did CPR for about ten minutes before you came back."

"Yeah, well, I didn't really go anywhere. My spirit or soul or whatever watched the whole thing."

"I've heard of that happening! Did you see a white light at the end of a tunnel?" Crystal interjected. Christopher raised his eyebrows. "Oh, sorry, keep going," she encouraged.

"Well, Michael came and Johnny came and they had a fight. Both of them had swords, and they were swinging them around trying to kill each other, I think. They weren't human, though. They were like aliens with wings or something. Michael was huge and glowing bright white. Johnny was even scarier. He was very angry and his face got really ugly and evil looking. He was spitting as he talked and was like the opposite of Michael, who was really calm about the whole thing. I am pretty sure no one else saw it but me. I saw the firefighters cutting me out of the car and

I saw the paramedics doing CPR and loading me into the ambulance, but not one of them looked over to where I was standing—or my spirit was standing—watching this sword fight. I heard voices—yours and Tony's and Terry's and even Cathy's, I think. I couldn't tell what you were saying, but whatever it was, it was giving Michael courage and power. Just before I went back into my body, Michael rammed the sword through Johnny's chest and he disappeared. There was smoke and a rotten egg smell. It was pretty gruesome."

"It sounds horrible!" whispered Crystal. "I'm so sorry you had that experience."

"No, no, it wasn't all horrible," said Christopher. "When it was just me and Michael at the end of the fight, I felt Heaven."

"Felt Heaven? You didn't see it? No bright light at the end of a tunnel?"

"No…" Christopher thought carefully about what he wanted to say. "I didn't see it. Michael was standing in the way with his sword out. But I felt it. It's hard to describe. The only words that even come close are love, peace, overwhelming joy. I didn't want to come back, Crystal. I wanted to die and go to Heaven. I wanted to be with the one who loved me that much—so much that I felt overwhelmed by it. I didn't want it to stop."

"Oh," said Crystal. "So why did you? Come back, I mean."

"I don't think Michael thought I was ready to go. He looked like he was guarding the door."

"Oh," said Crystal.

"He said I'm the last one." Christopher looked intently at Crystal. Would she think he had gone too far? That he was crazy? Or that the brain trauma had caused hallucinations?

"That had something to do with why they were fighting," Christopher added slowly, hoping Crystal would understand because he sure didn't. "Michael said I'm the last one. God is waiting for me to choose life or death so He could come back and then all of His people would get to go home. I was pretty sure God's vote was for me to choose life. But maybe I was wrong. I wanted to die, but I guess I actually chose life because I came back. I chose to live and nothing has happened."

"Geez!" Crystal exclaimed. "That's a lot of pressure on you!"

"Right?" Christopher said. "I mean, how do I know that whole thing was real? It could have just been my brain making things up because it was dying."

Crystal took both Christopher's hands in hers and stood up. "I don't know, Chris. It sounds real. The Bible talks about angels fighting, and God certainly does love you. Satan hates God and hates people because they are made in God's image and because God loves us. The Bible says Satan is like a lion prowling around looking for people to devour. Devour. That's a pretty strong word."

"Oh yeah—Michael also told me to find Jesus. That was the last thing he said—find Jesus."

"Oh, that's easy," said Crystal. "I can introduce you."

CHAPTER 28

T rue to her word, the next morning Crystal stopped by
with a Bible and gave it to Christopher.

"This book tells you all about Jesus. You can meet Him
by reading it and being open to what it has to tell you
about Him. Don't close off your mind just because you hate
religion, OK? Really read it." Crystal directed him.

"KO," said Christopher. "I mean, O-K," he said slowly.
"I'll try, but it's been hard for me to read anything since the
accident. My brain gets so tired and the words look blurry."

"Oh," said Crystal, "I didn't think about that. Well, I can
read to you, if you'd like."

"Sure," said Christopher, closing his eyes.

Crystal opened to the book of John and began reading.
Christopher didn't understand all the words, but he enjoyed
hearing Crystal's voice. It was sweet, and peaceful. He had
sure been stupid to let her go. He wondered if she was still
dating Tony and opened his mouth to ask her when she
paused to turn the page.

"Crystal, stickily you gopher watch?" is what came out
of his mouth.

She looked at him, puzzled. "What?" she asked.

Christopher took a deep breath and tried again, this time speaking much more slowly. "Are—you—still—with—Tony?"

Crystal closed the Bible with her finger holding her place. "I'm not going out with anyone right now, but Tony and I are still friends."

Christopher smiled. Perhaps he had a chance. He reached out and took her hand. She pulled it away slowly.

"Christopher, I don't want to date anyone right now. I need to concentrate on school and my life and, most importantly, on my relationship with Jesus. I want to do what is right."

Christopher stared at her. "Are you… are you an angel too? Like Michael? Or maybe like Johnny? Gosh, is everyone around me an alien?" He pulled the sheet over his head and closed his eyes. "Just go away. I'm losing my mind."

"I'm not an angel, Chris, or an alien. I'm just me."

"Go away."

"But…"

"Go away!" Christopher couldn't think. His head was pounding. All he wanted to do was sleep. When there was no response, he opened his eyes and pulled the sheet away from his face. Crystal was gone, but she had left the Bible on the table near his bed. He sighed and buzzed the nurse.

"I have a wicked headache," he told her. "I need morphine."

"Good timing," she said. "I was just bringing you your meds." The nurse injected the morphine into his IV. "We'll need to wean you off your pain medications soon so you can go home. You should be good to go in a few days."

Christopher barely heard the last sentence. He was going to tell her "thank you" for the morphine, but he drifted off to sleep before he could get the words out.

The dreams without the morphine had been horrifying, so he was grateful for the empty darkness of drugged sleep. He hadn't told Crystal his dreams, and he didn't plan to. He didn't plan to tell anyone. They were too ghastly.

When he closed his eyes, he could see them. Hundreds of ghoulish faces grinning and leering at him from the sky. Their eyes were absolute evil—dark and full of a vicious desire for their prey. Scars marked their faces like river valleys and ridges on a topography map. They were all cackling at him gleefully with twisted open mouths, the cacophonous sound growing louder and louder in his head. Their bird-like claws reached hungrily for him, but there was an invisible line they couldn't seem to cross to actually get to him. They came closer and closer each night he dreamed them. In his dream, he was frozen in place. Frozen with fear, unable to move or run away or even cry out. He was sure one of these nights they would cross that imaginary line and devour him.

The drugs helped. As long as they were in his system, he could keep the dreams at bay. Once they wore off, the demons returned. He would wake in the middle of the night, soaked in sweat, heart racing. He would count the hours and minutes until he would be allowed more morphine. Morphine to still the voices. Morphine to still the fear. Morphine to still the dreams. He was afraid when the nurse said he would not have morphine when he went home. He desperately needed the drugs to continue.

In the morning, Christopher called TJ.

"Hey, TJ, what's up?" Christopher tried to sound cheerful and rested.

"Chris? Hey buddy, I heard you were in a pretty bad wreck. Too bad about your car. I know how much you loved her. But, hey, how're you doing?" TJ's southern drawl was soft and distant.

"Oh, I've been better," Christopher said. "That's why I'm calling. I need you to hook me up with some pain killers. The doctors are letting me go home tomorrow and they won't give me any. They said I should be fine with just Tylenol. Tylenol! Shit! That doesn't even touch the pain I'm in."

TJ was paying attention now. "Sure, sure, I can do that," he said. "I can get you some Oxy. It's a great pain killer—better than morphine."

"That's great. That's great. When? How, how soon can you get it?" Christopher was getting fidgety.

"I'll have it for you tomorrow. It may be expensive," TJ warned. "It's not that easy to get."

"Whatever it is, I'll pay it," Christopher said. "I'll text you when I'm home. You can come by say, early evening?"

"Yeah, no problem." TJ was happy to have a new customer. Oxycodone was actually not all that difficult to find in one form or another, but if he said it was, he could charge extra. He was a little short on cash this semester, so bringing

Christopher into the fold would be good for business and good for his wallet. Besides, this rich kid could afford it.

He whistled a happy tune as he walked up the front steps of Christopher's house the next day. It was just before 7:00 p.m. and already dark. He pulled his coat collar up around his neck and knocked.

"Hello TJ," said Teresa, opening the door. "Christopher said you might stop by. It sure is good to see you. I think Christopher needs some friends about now. He seems a bit depressed," she confided. "How's school going this semester?"

"It's going great, Mrs. D'Antoni." TJ put on his best manners. "Thank you. I sure do miss your son, though. He was a good roommate. How is he doing?"

"Oh, physically he's healing. The concussion was a bad one, though. He mixes up his words and stutters sometimes, but that's nothing. He'll get over that I'm sure. Come on in and he can tell you himself."

Teresa led the way into the living room where Christopher was sprawled on the couch flipping channels on the TV. He sat up when he saw TJ and beckoned him over, trying to appear cool and calm as he struggled to stand up. His leg was healing, but still stiff from lack of use over the past month.

"Well, now, it looks like Christopher is excited to see you," said Teresa. "His other friends have not been able to come around yet, so I'm sure he's been lonely with just me and his dad for company. I'll be right back with some sodas.

Oh, TJ, would you prefer sweet tea? Is that what they drink where you're from? I think I could make some if you'd like."

"Yes, Ma'am, it is, but soda will be just fine," said TJ, amused. "Thank you, Mrs. D'Antoni."

Christopher shifted his weight from foot to foot. "We'll take soda. Thanks, Mom." He was impatient for her to leave the room so he could get down to business with TJ.

"Do you have it?" Christopher asked TJ as soon as his mother was out of hearing range.

"Sure do. Do you have the money?" TJ drawled.

"Yes, yes." Christopher reached into his pocket and thrust a handful of bills toward TJ. "Hurry, hurry. She'll be back soon. It doesn't take that long to get soda."

"Here you go." TJ dangled the plastic bag of pills in front of his face. Christopher snatched it from him and shoved it into his pocket as his mother came back in to the room carrying a tray with two cans of soda, glasses with ice, and an assortment of cookies. She set it on the coffee table.

"Here you go, boys," she said. "Don't stay too long though, TJ, OK? Christopher still gets tired pretty fast." She poured soda into the glasses and handed them to the boys. The tinkling ice annoyed Christopher. He needed TJ to go and his mother to stop being so, so…motherly.

TJ took a long slow drink from his glass, then set it back down on the tray.

"I can't stay tonight anyway," TJ told her. "I've got a test tomorrow that I have to finish studying for. I just wanted to come by and see how my friend was doing. Glad you're doing better, Chris." TJ gave Teresa a kiss on the cheek and shook Christopher's hand. "I'll come back another time to check up on you," he told him, winking.

"Yeah, sure, sure," said Christopher nervously, his hand in his pocket. "Come back in a few days."

"Alrighty then," said TJ. "See you soon."

CHAPTER 29

After TJ left, it was easy to convince his parents that he was tired and just needed some alone time in his room. They had been hovering since bringing him home from the hospital. His mother actually came in to his room to tuck him in. She hadn't done that since he was about ten or eleven. But, he let her do it as he yawned and pretended to doze off. He kept his eyes shut as he heard her walk across the room and quietly close his door. He waited a few minutes, then opened his eyes and reached under his pillow for the pills.

TJ hadn't told him how many to take, so Christopher figured he would try one and, if that didn't do the trick, he could take another. He tossed one in his mouth and swallowed it with a drink of water from the glass his mother had left near his bedside.

He needed a better place to hide the pills. He was sure his mother would find them when she made his bed in the morning if he left them under his pillow. Christopher looked around his room. A dresser drawer? No. His mother did his laundry and put his clothes away. The bedside table? No. Too obvious. Under the mattress? No. Again, too obvious. His father kept porn magazines under his own mattress so that would be the first place he'd look if he suspected Christopher of anything. Maybe in the Tylenol bottle? He could put them underneath the Tylenol or dump the Tylenol completely. No. If his mother thought he needed pain medication, she would get the Tylenol bottle and notice the pills were not Tylenol. Shit! Shit! Shit! Why hadn't he thought this through? He sat on his bed and stared straight ahead.

The Bible! It was on his bookshelf, right in front of him. He could put the pills in the Bible. No one in his family would pick it up to read it. Perfect! Christopher pulled the Bible off the shelf and flipped the pages until he reached what he thought was the middle. P-S-A-L-M 121, he read. Then he read some more. And more. This seemed like someone was sending him a message. If only it were true, he thought.

"My help comes from the Lord," he read in a whisper. This is cool, he thought. God doesn't sleep. God watches over me night and day. God keeps me from harm and watches over my life. Uh oh, it says God watches me coming and going. Does that mean He sees me now? Sees what I am doing now?

Christopher put the plastic envelope with the five remaining pills in the Bible where he had been reading and quickly shut it. He put the Bible back on the shelf and crawled into bed. The pill he took was starting to make him feel very relaxed and drowsy. He would not worry about the message in the Bible tonight. He could always think about it tomorrow. He was feeling good right now. TJ was right. This was way better than morphine.

No dreams haunted him that night. He slept through until morning and woke up feeling more rested than he had since before the accident. That just confirmed for him that taking the Oxy was what he was supposed to do. It was not wrong.

Teresa smiled when she heard Christopher singing in the shower. Her boy was back! She had been so worried she might lose him during those weeks in the hospital. Why would God give her a miracle baby and then take him away? She had prayed and prayed in the first few days after the accident. It had felt odd, praying. She had been content to let the priest do the praying for her all her life. Yet, there she was, trying to talk to God herself—as if He would listen to her! It brought her comfort, though, even if she wasn't sure God actually heard her. But, then again, maybe He had heard her! Christopher was alive and getting better every day. His singing was proof of that. Surely.

Her family was intact and back together again. Joseph and Christopher were her whole world. Well, almost. Johnny and Michael had also been a part of that world for such a long time, too. She wondered where they were and why they had not come to see Christopher after his accident. She had texted them both to let them know what happened but had not heard back from either one, which was odd. They adored Christopher as much as she did. And he had enjoyed having two big brothers. Teresa wondered if they had had an argument or something. Christopher had not said anything, but he had been off to college and then this… They must have just grown apart, Teresa thought to herself. But she missed having them around. She would have to reach out and invite them for dinner when Johnny got back from Turkey.

Christopher was charming and relaxed at dinner the second night home. He knew those pills were waiting for him, so he wasn't anxious about sleeping or dreaming. He would take another one tonight to banish the nightmare. Hopefully, he wouldn't need the pills forever, but for now they were helping him.

"So, Christopher, I haven't seen Johnny or Michael for a while. Did you guys have a fight or something?" Joseph asked, scooping a spoonful of mashed potatoes onto his plate.

Teresa kicked him under the table. "Ouch! What was that for?" he growled at her, passing the potatoes to Christopher.

The words "Johnny," "Michael," and "fight" triggered a flashback in Christopher's mind. For a second, he saw clashing swords and giant aliens with wings. He choked on the food he had just put in his mouth and started coughing. Teresa jumped up and frantically patted his back.

"Are you all right Christopher? See what you did Joseph? You should not have brought up their names. Breathe! Breathe!"

"What? I just asked about Johnny and Michael. What's wrong with that?" Joseph said over the noise of the coughing and Teresa's scolding. "Suddenly they're not part of our family anymore?"

Christopher gradually stopped coughing. "I'm OK, Ma. Really. It just went down the wrong pipe, that's all."

"We—your father and I—were thinking that maybe something happened between you and Johnny and Michael. You had such a good time in Turkey with Johnny and then… nothing. They seem to have just disappeared from our lives. Your father didn't mean to upset you. We're worried, that's all." Teresa looked so sad. She really did love Johnny and Michael as if they were her own sons.

Teresa and Joseph stared at Christopher, waiting. His parents were good at this. They would be all sympathetic and interested and focus intently on him until he spilled his guts. Not this time. No way. But he would have to say something or the staring contest would continue indefinitely.

"I didn't fight with them," Christopher said. "But I think they fought with each other. They're probably just cooling off somewhere and will come back when they've worked it out." He thought basing his story on the truth might work, even if he bent that truth a little.

"Do you think that's why Johnny went back to Turkey? To be with his other brothers?" Teresa asked intently.

"Well, he certainly got along well with them, so maybe," said Christopher. If he let his mother believe she was right, she would let it drop.

"I wonder where Michael went then," she said.

"To his father," said Christopher without thinking.

"His father? He finally told you about his father?" Now Joseph was interested too. "The deadbeat?"

"Oh, I don't really know. I'm just guessing," said Christopher, trying to cover up his blunder. "If Johnny went to his brothers for support, then maybe Michael went to his father to get him on his side." Christopher knew he was talking too much. He did that when he was lying or making things up.

"Yeah, yeah, that's probably it. Johnny had his two brothers—maybe more siblings, who knows—so he went there to prove he was right about...whatever. Michael had no one so he went to his deadbeat dad to get some sympathy or to get Johnny in trouble or something."

"Hmm," said Teresa.

"Hmm," said Joseph. He knew a bullshit story when he heard one and he'd just heard one. If Christopher wasn't going to rat on his friends, he would respect that. It sounded like they both were in trouble—jail maybe? In his experience, that was usually the reason people just disappeared. Jail or dead. He doubted they were dead. Christopher would be upset about that. But jail, not so much. Christopher had seen relatives come and go from prisons since he was born. It was a way of life for those connected to the D'Antoni family. Not something to be proud of, but still...it happened.

"OK, then," Joseph told him. "Your mom is going to clean up the dishes and I'm going to read the paper and have a cigar. You want one?"

"No thanks, Dad. I think I'll go to my room and rest for a bit." Christopher was looking forward to that pill.

"OK. Good night," Joseph told him, getting up from the table.

"Good night, Christopher," said his mother, collecting the dishes and taking them out to the kitchen. "Don't forget to brush your teeth."

Christopher rolled his eyes. "I'm not five, Ma. I know to brush my teeth."

Teresa laughed. "I know. I know. But you'll always be my baby." She kissed the top of his head and picked up his plate. "Off you go."

Christopher left the table and hurried to his bedroom. He shut the door and took the Bible off the shelf. The pills were still there. He popped one in his mouth and swallowed, flipping through the pages. He had not been thrilled with what he had read yesterday, so perhaps there was a better place in the Bible to keep the pills so he wouldn't have to keep seeing the part that God watched his every move when he wanted another dose of Oxy. That was kind of creepy.

Christopher thought maybe an inch or so more toward the front of the Bible would work. He ended up in the part of the book that was 1 Samuel 2. Perfect. He would just glance at the words to make sure there was nothing creepy in this part.

"Why do you do such things? I hear about these wicked deeds of yours," jumped off the page.

Christopher slammed the book shut. First the dreams, now this? He felt like he was definitely going crazy. He popped another pill in his mouth and then one more for good measure and then shoved the two that were left between the Bible and another book on his shelf. He would look for a different hiding place in the morning.

CHAPTER 30

Christopher was just dozing off in a euphoric haze when he caught a flash of light through his closed eyes. No. Not again. He was not going to open his eyes. Keep them shut. Keep them shut. Keep them shut. It will go away. Go away.

A chuckle echoed in his head. He heard a voice—Johnny's voice—say, "Keep up the good work kid." Then, a split second before the next flash of light, he was gone.

Christopher opened his eyes just enough to see but not enough for anyone watching to know he was awake. He saw Michael with his sword in hand, looking out the window before he, too, disappeared.

A wave of nausea hit and Christopher jumped out of bed and raced to the bathroom. He knelt in front of the toilet and vomited into the bowl over and over again. Exhausted, he lay face down on the cool bathroom tile floor and slept.

Johnny relaxed in a lounge chair on a Cuban beach with a cigar in one hand and a fancy alcoholic drink in the other hand. It had an umbrella perched on the inside, stuck with a toothpick on a piece of pineapple. Peter and Julian joined him, grumbling.

"Why are we here? What is it you want? You messed up and now you want us to help you again?" Peter was being snarky. He didn't care. He hated Johnny, and he hated being summoned.

"Have a seat." Johnny gestured to the two lounge chairs next to him. Each chair also had a drink waiting for them in side cupholders. Julian plopped down into one of the chairs and drained his drink in one gulp. Peter sulked and stood there with his arms crossed.

"I asked you here," Johnny said, emphasizing asked. "Because I thought you would want to know what I have discovered. It might help you in the future."

"You think you can teach us something? You—who failed at the biggest mission over two thousand years ago?" Julian was not impressed.

"You failed in the last big mission. That's why I was chosen for this one. Just saying," Johnny smirked. "Your failure almost ruined everything. It certainly makes victory more difficult. We've been trying to clean up your mess ever since, so I would shut up if I were you."

"You just want to gloat? Is that it?" Peter was still sulking. "You have nothing to gloat about. You failed."

"No, no I did not. Things are going quite well, actually." Johnny was grinning. "Who knew that I really didn't have to try so hard after all. Left alone, humans have a knack of messing up their lives all by themselves. I just have to step back and let it happen. Voila. Done. Success."

"What are you talking about?" Julian asked, irritated. "We have to trick them, lie to them, cause arguments, teach them about pleasure so they forget everything else…"

"Nope. No, we do not. They are drawn to pleasure, greed, selfishness, all on their own. For example," Johnny said dramatically, "I tried for years to get Christopher to try drugs. What better way to guide a person to Hell than to cloud their minds with drugs so they live for nothing else? But, it didn't work, as you know. He was adamantly against drugs, even when I made sure his roommate was a drug dealer! But, after I left, he found out the pleasure of drugs all on his own. I didn't have to do a thing." Johnny closed his eyes, smiling, and took another sip of his drink.

"Give us some credit," said Julian. "We introduced him to pleasure. Don't forget the hookah and the girls and the raki. He got a taste of it from us and then wanted more. That was us."

Johnny grunted. He wasn't giving them credit for any of it.

"See what I did?" Johnny showed them a picture of Christopher passed out on the bathroom floor. "Me. All me. Just by leaving him to his own devices—and keeping Michael out of the way. He's been chasing me all over the world," Johnny said with a cunning smile.

Michael wasn't sure where Johnny had gone. However, Johnny wasn't with Christopher, so that was a relief. His mission was to protect Christopher's life until it was Time. He had thought for years that keeping Johnny at bay was central to that mission but now he wasn't sure. He would have to check back in with the Father. But first, he blew gently in the air above Teresa's sleeping face, causing a cold breeze that would wake her. It was too late to appear on their doorstep and ring the bell. He would have to do this another way.

Teresa stirred. Invisible, Michael blew again. This time Teresa sat up and shook Joseph awake.

"Joseph, something's wrong. I can feel it."

Joseph turned over, intending to go back to sleep.

"I'm going to check on Christopher," she said.

Teresa got out of bed and tiptoed down the hallway to Christopher's room. She opened the door and peered in. His bed was empty. It had been slept in, though. The sheets were in disarray and the quilt was on the floor. There was a light in the bathroom. Teresa knocked but did not get an answer. It was unlocked. She opened it just a little and gasped in horror.

"Christopher!" Teresa threw open the door and knelt by her son, shaking him. He did not respond. There was vomit all over the floor near the toilet.

"Joseph! Come quickly. Something's wrong with Christopher!" Teresa shouted in panic, as loud as she could or had ever done. She was not the shouting type and her vocal cords were not used to the demands she was making of them now. The adrenaline and panic joined forces so that Teresa's shout carried to the far end of the house. Joseph came running, but Christopher didn't appear to notice her, the shouting, or anything else. Drool slid down his chin.

He was breathing, Teresa was relieved to see, but it was ragged and shallow. Joseph came stumbling in, half awake and confused by the commotion.

"Oh my god," Joseph said, now fully awake and noticing his son sprawled in vomit on the floor. "I'll be right back." He knew exactly what this was. He had seen it before with some of his cousins. He had not expected it in his own family, but he was prepared. He was always prepared.

Joseph ran back into the room with Narcan and quickly administered it, just in case. Christopher moaned and grabbed Joseph's wrist.

"What…what…are…you…doing?" he croaked. "Let me have this…"

"We need to call 9-1-1," said Teresa, crying.

"No. We call 9-1-1, they call the cops. My boy is not going to jail for this. I'll call Vinny. He knows a doctor that will come to the house all confidential like. Let's get him up."

Joseph and Teresa lifted Christopher to his feet and held him up, forcing him to walk with them around the house. Joseph picked up his cell phone from the kitchen counter as they went by and dialed Vinny. He quickly explained the situation.

"Yeah, we're keeping him walking and awake. Get the doc here as fast as you can. Got that?" Joseph hung up without waiting for an answer. Vinny would do what he asked. He had no doubt about that. If anything happened to Christopher, Vinny would not want to take the blame.

CHAPTER 31

C hristopher was angry. He wasn't sure why he was angry, but the rage was there, deep inside and bubbling to the surface. He had a splitting headache and his mouth felt like he was sucking on cotton balls. He scratched his arms and neck and legs and tried to reach his back. His skin felt like it was super dry and itched all over. He glared at his mother as she brought in a tray full of options for breakfast.

"I'm not hungry!" he snapped at her. "You're treating me like a baby. I'm not your baby. I'm a full grown-ass man. Leave me alone!"

"Fine," she said putting the tray down on his dresser. "But I'll leave this here just in case you get hungry later."

Teresa went out. The doctor and his father came in.

"How are you feeling, son?" asked the doctor. "That was quite a scare you gave your parents last night."

"I'm fine," growled Christopher. "Nothing wrong with me. You can go now." He needed to see if those two pills were still on his shelf.

"Not yet," said his father. "I need to know what you took and where you got it."

"Just some pain meds, and I'm not telling you anything else so goodbye."Christopher was being rude and disrespectful. He knew it and he didn't care. All he cared about was finding those pills and escaping the hell that was taking over his mind.

"You know we have ways of making people talk. I never thought I'd have to use them on my own son," Joseph threatened.

"You'd never hurt me," Christopher laughed. "I'm the miracle boy."

"I've never hurt you yet," said Joseph. "There's always a first time. You can't disrespect your father, boy."

Christopher looked into his father's eyes and saw icy, steel, emotionless determination. He was not kidding. Christopher shuddered inside. He had never seen the side of his father he was seeing now. This was the D'Antoni king, the D'Antoni mob boss, not his dad. He gulped.

"Uh, uh, OK. It was Oxy. I just took three pills. I'm still in a lot of pain, Dad," he whimpered. "The accident took a lot out of me. I need them."

The doctor and Joseph exchanged glances.

"Where did you get the Oxy, Christopher?" asked the doctor. It may have been mixed with something that was unsafe."

"From…from a friend," said Christopher slowly.

"TJ?" asked his father. "Your mother said TJ was here and then left abruptly. Sounds like a drug deal to me."

Christopher just nodded, hating to give his friend up, but hating even more the thought of being hurt by one of his father's thugs.

"I'll take care of that," said his father. "TJ won't be coming here anymore. You'll be fine by tomorrow."

"But, Dad, I really need…"

"Christopher," interrupted the doctor, "You are allergic to whatever it was you took. That's why you are itching so much. And you took too much of it. I can prescribe something for you that will help, but you have to take it exactly as prescribed, not handfuls at a time."

Christopher sighed in relief. "OK. No problem. I will."

"Yes, you will," said his father. "Because your mother will give you the medicine when it is time for it and in the proper dosage. You will not have free access."

"But…"

"No buts. That's the way it will be."

Christopher didn't dare argue. He had really won anyway. They believed that he was still in pain, and he was getting pills he didn't have to pay for. Perfect. He closed his eyes. The corners of his mouth turned up in a slow smile.

When Joseph and the doctor left the room, Christopher listened carefully to make sure no one else was coming in. He got out of bed and tiptoed to his bookshelf. He pulled out the Bible. Great! The two pills were still there, shoved in the back half hidden behind another book. He would save the pills just in case the doctor's prescription didn't work.

In his haste to reach them, he dropped the Bible. He cringed and then listened carefully to make sure no one had heard the thump. He did not need anyone to come running to make sure he was OK and see what he had gripped tightly in his fist.

The Bible was open on the floor. Oh, what now, Christopher thought. Another message? He was getting superstitious. But he couldn't help himself from looking, just to see.

The Bible had fallen open to a book called James. He picked up the Bible with his eyes closed, then quickly and bravely opened them as he thrust a finger in the middle of the page. He read, "Why, you do not even know what will happen tomorrow. What is your life? You are a mist that appears for a little while and then vanishes."

Christopher threw the Bible across the room. He didn't care who heard it.

CHAPTER 32

T J stopped by the next day. He heard his mother answer the door and tell TJ to go away, that he wasn't welcome in their home anymore. He heard the door shut and a car squeal away a few minutes later. If he needed more Oxy, he would have to find another way to get it. For now, the doctor's prescription was working, thank God. Or thank his good luck, anyway. His pills had disappeared. Christopher was pretty sure his mother had found them and flushed them, but he didn't have proof, and he didn't dare ask.

"Time to go!" his mother called to him from the kitchen.

Physical therapy was three times a week. To his surprise, Christopher actually enjoyed it. He was strengthening the muscles in his leg now that the cast was off.

"Tony's picking you up today after therapy," his mother said. "He asked if he could, and that would help me out, so I said yes. He seems like a good boy," she added.

"Tony?" Christopher hadn't seen Tony in months—since right before the accident actually. Tony made him feel uncomfortable with all his Jesus talk. He was always weird, but now, well, he was really weird. At least, that's what Christopher wanted to think. Tony had changed, for sure, but if Christopher was honest, the changes were all good. He could still be annoying, but instinctively Christopher knew he could trust him, could tell him anything without being judged. No matter how many times Christopher rebuffed him, Tony kept coming back. Tony had thought they were friends ever since middle school and now—well, now, Christopher supposed they actually were friends. Or could be friends. He needed friends.

Christopher limped out of the therapy building and saw Tony waiting in the parking lot. He got in the car and shut the door.

"Hey, man. Good to see you. How are you doing?" Tony asked.

"I'm good, Tony. Haven't seen you around in a while." Christopher pointed out. "Where've you been?"

Usually chatty Tony was silent.

"Hey, Tony, what's up?" Christopher asked him, concerned.

"Let's get some coffee and talk," said Tony.

He pulled into the parking lot of The Daily Planet, a diner not far from Christopher's therapy building. They went inside and sat in a booth near the back where it was quiet.

"I'm so sorry, Chris," said Tony in hushed tones after the waitress brought their coffee. "I think the accident was my fault and I couldn't face you. I almost got my best friend killed and I just couldn't deal with that."

"Your fault? Tony, I was hit by a pickup truck, not you. None of us knew the driver. It was just some random guy.

How do you figure the accident was your fault? If anything, it was mine since I went through a yellow light without looking. I wasn't paying attention." Christopher had no idea what Tony was talking about.

"I should have been with you. Crystal and I bailed on you and let you go home by yourself. If I was in the car, I might have seen the truck coming and warned you."

"If you had been with me, you might have been killed," Christopher pointed out. "He hit the passenger side of the car."

"But I should have been there," Tony insisted. "And because I wasn't…"

"You think you could have prevented this?" Christopher asked.

Tony nodded. "Maybe," he said.

"And because you didn't prevent it, you think that means you caused it?" Christopher shook his head and frowned. "Tony, that makes no sense."

"Well, if you put it that way, I guess not. I still feel guilty though."

"Look, Tony, I absolve you from all responsibility, OK?" Christopher laughed and made the sign of the cross in the air as he had seen Father Giovanni do. "It was not your fault. I don't blame you—never blamed you. Your mere presence does not protect me."

"You were angry at us when you left. I'm guessing that was what was distracting you." Tony had his head down, both hands around his coffee cup.

"Nah," said Christopher, "Well, actually, it was the topic you guys were talking about, not really the people, that I was thinking about. But you can't blame the accident on that either. It was just an accident."

"OK," said Tony, leaning back in the booth and taking a sip of coffee.

"Tony, do you really believe that crap about Jesus flying a space ship back to the earth someday? You've gotta admit that is pretty weird." Christopher tried to mask his interest by holding his coffee cup up to his mouth and blowing in it. "Geez, this is hot," he said.

"I believe Jesus is coming back one day—probably soon. Probably not in a space ship since that's not the way He left. All the signs are there that we can expect Him soon."

"Signs? What signs?" Christopher was more curious than he wanted to let on.

"Well," Tony said, holding up his index finger. "One, the Bible says that Israel will become a nation in one day—that happened on May 14, 1948."

Tony continued holding up fingers as he counted through the signs he knew. "Two, there will be a falling away of the church—that happened with the Covid pandemic. People stopped going to church. Three, there will be more 'pestilence'—you know about Covid and Monkey Pox and Polio showing up a couple of years ago. Four, human knowledge will greatly increase—look at our technology and how we can Google anything we want to know. Five, people will travel throughout the whole world—people have been doing that for a while now."

Tony released his grip on his coffee cup so he could continue counting with his other hand. "Six, the earth will be filled with violence—definitely happening after the defunding the police movement, with cities seeing an increase of violent crime. We've had world wars and acts of terrorism like 9-11. Russia started a war with Ukraine that has pulled in other nations in one way or another. Or…the Russian thing could be one of the ten world leaders starting to gobble up three of the other leaders, like it says in the book of Revelation. Then there is the war between China and Taiwan, and between North and South Korea. I'm sure there are more I don't even know about!

"Oh yeah," Tony continued, holding up a seventh finger, "Another sign is that Israel will rebuild the temple. They've already laid the foundation for the third temple and are putting up the walls as we speak. They've had the items for inside the temple for years now. Then there is the economics situation—number eight. Eventually there will be a world-wide financial system. That could be crypto currency or something else coming, but it's coming."

Christopher put his coffee cup down. "The Bible really says all that?"

"Yes," said Tony.

"And you believe it?"

"I've seen it coming true, so yes, I believe it."

"Is there anything left to happen before, you know, Jesus comes back?" Christopher asked. He was going to use his skills in logic to make Tony admit that the signs couldn't be true because Jesus hadn't come back, had He.

Tony thought for a minute. "Well, I'm not an expert in exactly what happens when, but the Bible says something about young men seeing visions and old men dreaming. Other than that, no, I don't think so."

"Dreaming?" Christopher sat up straight, his plan to trap Tony in a web of logic instantly forgotten. "Just old men, though, right?"

"That's what it says," replied Tony. "Why?"

"What is a vision? What does that mean?" Christopher asked.

"It's, uh, seeing things others don't see, I think. Things that are true."

Now it was Christopher's turn to be silent.

"Chris, Chris!" Tony waved a hand in front of Christopher's face. "You there?"

"Yeah, I'm here. Not that I believe all that stuff, but I may have…I may have seen a…seen a…vision."

"Cool!" said Tony. "What did you see?"

"It's not cool," said Christopher. "I don't want to see things. It makes me feel like I'm crazy."

"Tell me what you saw and I'll tell you if you're crazy," joked Tony.

When Christopher remained silent, Tony said, "Seriously, man. You can tell me. I won't think you're crazy."

"Crystal didn't tell you anything?" Christopher asked.

"No, man. If you told her anything in confidence, she wouldn't breathe a word of it to anybody. She's loyal that way."

"Oh," said Christopher, stalling.

Tony waited.

"When I was in the accident and the paramedics were giving me CPR, I saw two angels sword fighting. They looked just like Michael and Johnny. The one that looked like Johnny went away, but I had a conversation with the one that looked like Michael. He talked about God and stuff like I was on my deathbed and being given a second chance."

"That's cool!" Tony was impressed.

"But later, when I was in the hospital and getting better, I saw some pretty nasty stuff every time I dreamed," Christopher told him. "Gruesome faces and sharp claws coming for me. I had that dream almost every night. It scared me shitless. The only way I could keep the dream from coming was by taking drugs."

"The doctors gave you something for it?" Tony asked.

"No. They didn't know. I didn't think it was a good idea to tell them. I got the drugs from TJ—you know, my old roommate. Turns out he's a drug dealer. That's how he makes money to stay in college."

Tony was stunned. Christopher had always been so adamant about staying away from drugs and so judgmental of those who didn't.

"I don't get it," said Tony, confused. "You bought drugs from a drug dealer? Why the heck would you do that? It was just a dream. You wake up, you're fine."

"It felt like more than a dream." Christopher was beginning to get defensive. "It felt real—as if I could see something in an alien world that others couldn't see."

Tony backed down a little. He wanted his friend to keep talking so he nodded his head and waited for him to continue. Crystal had told him that Christopher had wanted to meet Jesus. Perhaps that would happen today if he just listened first.

"It's like there are two opposing sides that couldn't be more different from each other. When I was talking to Michael—the Michael angel, I mean—I felt a God that was love, joy, and peace all rolled into a single emotion. It was awesome. He was awesome. But then, I wasn't allowed to stay, and I woke up in the hospital room. Since then I've only felt the danger and evil from those demons in my dreams. What do you think this means, Tony? Am I going crazy? This can't be real so it must be all in my head. It must be part of the traumatic brain injury, right? I'm afraid to say anything to the doctors. I think they would have me committed to an insane asylum."

Christopher paused and looked intently at Tony.

"Be honest," he told him.

"I've always been honest with you," Tony said. "And I don't think you're crazy. I think you've had real spiritual experiences."

"Yeah?" Christopher sounded relieved.

Tony nodded. "It sounds like there is a spiritual battle being fought over you, just like there is over all of us, only for some reason, you're being allowed to see it."

"Why, though? Why are they fighting? Why me?"

Tony shrugged. "I don't get a lot of it. I'm still learning." He paused, praying for the right words.

"But evidently you are important to both sides. You will need to choose sooner or later which side you will go with."

"Well, that's easy, Tony. Why would I ever choose the ugly, evil side that's trying to kill me? Of course I choose the other one!"

"Do you?" Tony let the question hang in the air.

The waitress came over to fill their coffee cups.

"Can I get you anything else?" she asked.

"No!" barked Christopher. Then, "Sorry, no thank you," he said in a nicer tone.

"Well, take all the time you need. We're not busy today," she said moving away from their table and on to the next one.

Christopher leaned forward and frowned. "Do you think I'm an idiot?" he asked Tony. "No one would choose the aliens trying to destroy them."

"People do, though," said Tony. "When they continue to do things that God has said not to do, they are choosing selfishness, greed, and all the things that those demons are offering them. When they turn away from God and ignore Him or when they won't admit they need God, or refuse to believe there is a God, they are choosing the other side."

Christopher couldn't immediately find an argument to counter Tony's point. Work, brain, work! This was the same nonsense he had heard and rejected when he went to that Bible study just before the accident.

"Ah, uh," he stuttered, "A person could just not choose either. Not take sides. Be Switzerland." He thought that was a pretty good argument. Many people believed that.

Tony shook his head. "You've seen the sides. You described them to me! There's good and there's evil. There's Heaven and there's Hell. Did you see a neutral place anywhere at anytime?"

Christopher kept his eyes down. "No," he said.

"No," repeated Tony slowly and firmly. "You will have to choose eventually, you know."

"Not today," said Christopher. "I'm still not sure I believe any of this so, not today."

CHAPTER 33

The following September brought the cool, crisp air that Teresa enjoyed so much. It was refreshing in a way, chasing away the heat of the summer with bursts of multi shades of reds and golds replacing the green landscape. She took a deep, long breath and ran down the front steps, smiling.

Christopher was back at college. She had worried about him over the past year—first the accident, then the drugs. Now, finally he seemed normal again. She and Joseph had offered to buy him another car to replace the Mustang, but he had refused. She understood that. He was probably afraid of being in another accident. They would give it a while longer.

Teresa was on her way to the women's Bible study at the corner church. They had been so supportive when Christopher was in the hospital, and she had made several friends there. She hadn't told Joseph where she went every Tuesday morning. He would not approve. His family were strict Catholics and to deviate even a little from that would send you to Hell, or so he thought. Teresa wasn't so sure about that anymore. She loved the Catholic church, the rituals, and the comfort of being assured she was forgiven of her sins after going to confession. But there was something missing. She couldn't put her finger on it, but she just knew that she was looking for something more. She felt that "something more" when she was with these friends, she just didn't know exactly what it was.

The ladies filled their cups with coffee or tea and sat at a round table in the church library. One of the women had made cookies and brought them to share. Teresa thought they were delicious! The conversations flowed smoothly as they talked about their children and grandchildren and things that had happened during the past week. Eventually, Judy, an older woman who seemed to know everyone, began the study portion of their morning.

"Did you ever feel like something was missing in your life?" she asked.

Teresa's ears perked up. That was exactly what she had been thinking about this morning!

Judy read from the Bible about the Samaritan woman who met Jesus at a well. She had been looking for that missing piece all her life and had tried to find it in men. For goodness sake—she had sex with at least five! That still didn't fill the hole in her heart, Judy told them. It wasn't until this woman met Jesus that she knew what the missing piece was. She needed a Savior—a personal relationship with God, not men.

"Now, men are fine," Judy joked. Everyone laughed.

"And friends are fine. But they can't give you the joy and peace and love like God can give you," she continued. "I love all of you, but I can't even come close to loving you the way God does." Judy paused for a minute, trying to think of a way to illustrate what these women needed to know.

"You were all talking about how much you loved your children. You would do anything for them." The women all nodded.

"How many of you have ever stepped in to get your child out of trouble? Or out of a punishment?"

All the hands went up.

"Once, my daughter was at a party where there was underage drinking," a woman named Delores said. "When I got there, the cops had already arrived and they were putting her in handcuffs. It was shocking! My baby in handcuffs! She was only 14. Anyway, I told the officer that he could take me to jail because I was the parent who let her come to the party. He didn't do that, but he must have felt sorry for me because he let her go."

"I sat in detention with my son once," said Maria, another member of the group. "There was no way I was going to let him take the punishment alone. He was only six!"

"Well, this is not about my kids, but I was very close with my older sister growing up," volunteered Paula. "I broke my mother's favorite coffee mug. My mother accused me of doing it, and when I didn't say anything, my sister stepped up and told my mother she would take the punishment. She got spanked with a belt." Paula paused for a moment before continuing.

"I think that brought us closer together because she saved me from that spanking. I know I loved her even more from that moment on."

Judy smiled. "That's a very good picture at what Jesus has done for all of us," she said. "We deserve punishment. All of us have sinned. But God, Jesus, took the punishment for us. How can we not love Him for that?"

The women were silent. Some were nodding. Some were thinking. Teresa felt a tear slide down her cheek and she quickly brushed it away.

"I can tell you that I wanted to know the Jesus that died for me so I started reading the Bible," Judy kept going. "I found out that He wants to know me, too. He wants a relationship with me. I told Him that I believed He died for me, that He rose again, and that He is in Heaven waiting for me. I told Him that I want to be His child, that I am committed to doing what He wants me to do, to living my life for Him instead of for me. I talk to Him every day through prayer. It's amazing. It has filled that missing piece in my heart."

Teresa wiped away another tear. "That's what I want, too," she whispered to herself. "Can I have that too?" she whispered a little louder.

The women held hands around the circle and Judy led them in prayer, giving an example of how they could pray to accept Jesus as Savior. Teresa said the words, emphasizing each one so God would know how serious she was about this. When she finished, she felt lighter somehow, happier.

As she picked up her head after the prayer, she thought for a minute that she saw Michael through the library window. Impossible! What would he be doing here? It must have been a shadow or her imagination. There was no one there.

Michael smiled and flew away.

Joseph had known Teresa was going to a different church every Tuesday morning and that she came home happy and content. He had her followed, just to be sure she wasn't having an affair. He didn't say anything to her about it, waiting for her to confess. When she didn't, he just kept watching. Watching and waiting. Waiting and watching. What was going on here?

He sometimes listened at the door of the church and heard an old lady talking about God and Jesus and religious stuff in the Bible. Joseph thought that was okay. His wife could do that if she wanted to. He just didn't know why she wouldn't tell him. He figured he'd better look into it.

Somewhere around the house there was a Bible. Joseph wanted to know what his wife was learning about. What about this book was making her so happy?

He searched for a Bible on Tuesday when Teresa was out of the house. He found one on Christopher's bookshelf, of all places! It was the one Michael had given him for his sixteenth birthday. Joseph opened it to the first page and started reading.

Just before Teresa was due home, Joseph put a bookmark in the page and left the house, the Bible tucked under the papers in his briefcase. He was surprised at how interesting this book was. He would need to read some more. He would definitely read some more. In fact, when he got to his office, he took the Bible out of his briefcase and continued reading, and reading, and reading. He found he could not put it down. He needed to know the end of the story.

Joseph didn't do any work that day. For the first time in his life, he read the whole book.

CHAPTER 34

That Saturday night, when Christopher was home for the weekend and Joseph had just finished his favorite dinner, Teresa poured the coffee and set out the dessert. She didn't sit down like she usually did. She stood, looking at them with her hands resting on the back of her chair.

"Sit, sit!" commanded Joseph. "What're you doing standing there staring? It's giving me the creeps. Sit!"

Teresa shook her head. "First, I've got to tell you something."

Joseph raised an eyebrow and looked at her in anticipation.

"I've been going to a Bible study at that church on the corner." She paused, expecting a comment or two from Joseph. When she didn't get one, she continued. "I accepted Jesus as my Savior this week. I believe Jesus is God and that He died for me. He loves me…"

Although her words petered out, her look was almost defiant, as if she were daring them to challenge her decision. Teresa pulled out her chair and sat down, waiting for whatever was coming next.

Christopher didn't say a word, but he thought he knew what was coming. His dad would laugh and tell her it was nonsense, that she was an emotional female in menopause. If that didn't work, he would begin shouting and cursing and demanding that she stop this craziness. He might even threaten her. It could turn into a real fight.

But none of that happened.

Joseph bowed his head and said nothing for a long time. Christopher could see that his mother was getting very nervous, but she was not backing down. She did not say, "never mind," or "I was just joking," or "pay no attention to me," or "what was I thinking?" She just sat there and looked back and forth from him to his father, expecting what, he didn't know.

"You chose a side?" Christopher blurted. Now, why did he say that? That would mean he believed there were sides, that what Tony told him was true. He didn't believe that. Did he believe that?

"I choose Jesus," she said.

Joseph picked up his head and looked at Teresa. He was very serious.

"Then, I do too," he said simply.

It was a simple statement, but not a simple decision. Christopher understood in a flash what that would mean for their family—the D'Antoni family.

"Dad?" Christopher asked. "You're the boss of this... family. If you become a Jesus freak, no one will listen to you anymore. You'll have no power, no influence. You're putting yourself in danger. You're putting us in danger! Someone will move in and take over. Who will that be, Dad, huh? Who's coming to kill us?"

Christopher was angry. What the heck? He slammed his fists on the table, pushed his chair back, and walked out of the room. He kept walking through the hallway and out the front door, slamming it behind him.

What was happening in his world? Everything was upside down and sideways. Having his parents choose a side was, well, there was no word for it except insane. It felt like everyone was against him. It felt like he was living in an alternate universe.

Christopher started running. He had to burn off this anger somehow. He felt like someone was backing him into a corner and he needed to escape. He would not choose. He would not choose. He would not choose.

"Leave me alone!" he shouted into the air. "All of you, leave me alone!"

Christopher did not see Terry before he ran into him.

"Whoa!" Terry barely managed to step to one side before they collided, taking the force of the crash mostly in his right shoulder. They grabbed on to each other to avoid falling.

"Sorry," mumbled Christopher, not looking up. He dropped his hands and was about to continue his run, but before he could take a step, Terry spoke.

"Hey, don't I know you? Chris, Christopher, right?" Terry asked.

"Yeah, that's me. You're...you're..."

"Terry," said Terry. "From the Bible study."

"Oh, of course you are," said Christopher sarcastically. "Who sent you to bump into me? God?"

"No," said Terry puzzled. "I run this route every morning. So…who sent you? God?"

"Geez!" Christopher said angrily. "Have a nice day." He didn't mean it. He ran for another five blocks before stopping, winded. Could he ever get away from this Jesus stuff? At night he dreamed of demons. During the day he was bombarded with Jesus nonsense. He sat down on the curb and put his head in his hands. He couldn't take this anymore. Something had to change.

Terry came and sat down on the curb next to him. He didn't speak. He just sat there with Christopher and prayed silently. He sensed a battle going on inside Christopher, he just didn't know how to help. Finally, Christopher spoke.

"I don't know what's going on," he said. "First Crystal and Tony, then my mom and dad. All into this Jesus mythology. What kind of power do you have over them? They must be hypnotized or something. There's no way my dad would have bought into this stuff in his right mind. Can't you just leave us alone so everything can go back to normal?" Christopher sounded a little whiny and desperate, but he didn't care.

Terry spoke quietly. "You know, there was a man named Saul a long, long time ago who was running from Jesus too. He wanted to do the right thing. He thought he was doing the right thing. He was not into the Jesus stuff and he persecuted and even killed people who were. He was as convinced as you that people who believed it were totally wrong and were tricking people into going the wrong way."

Christopher lifted his head just a little and glanced sideways at Terry. It was enough encouragement for Terry to continue.

"One day, on his way to arrest believers, he met Jesus in person. Jesus appeared to him and asked Saul why he was persecuting Him. When Saul asked Him who He was and the answer was 'Jesus', Saul had no more reason or excuse not to believe that He not only was real, but that He had lived, died, returned to life, and now was changed back to His godly form. The light surrounding Jesus blinded Saul. He had to wait three days for a miracle to get his sight back— that's how bright Jesus was. After that experience Saul became known as Paul and he was even more zealous about bringing people to Jesus than he had been about preventing them from knowing Jesus. He learned that the Jesus stuff was real. It changed his life. He never looked back and he never regretted it."

"So why doesn't Jesus appear to anyone else? It sounds like a baloney story to me. If Jesus is real, then I need to see Him."

"We will see Him one day. But, in the meantime, I feel His presence when I read the Bible and pray. I feel His presence when the wind blows and the leaves come out in the spring or when summer storms light up the sky. I see

Him in the smiles of children, in the kindness of strangers, and in the way He provides for my every need."

"Do you see Him in dreams or visions too?" Christopher tried to sound sarcastic, but it didn't quite come out that way. Terry took him seriously and tried to answer.

"God has used dreams to communicate with some people in the past," Terry told him. "And visions. Those methods will return in the last days."

"Last days?" Christopher was calmer now and his curiosity got the best of him. He really did want to know, even if he didn't believe it.

"The days right before Jesus returns to earth to gather up those who believe in Him. Those people will be caught up into the clouds to meet Him in the air. Sounds cool, right?"

Christopher nodded.

"Cool for those who believe," Terry continued. "But not cool for those left behind. That event—the rapture—allows evil to unleash a reign of terror on the earth for a few years before Jesus comes back with His army to destroy it and set up a new Heaven and a new earth. Those that are left here will see evil in a way they can't even imagine."

Christopher shuddered. He remembered the macabre faces in his dreams, screeching obscenities and reaching for him with poisonous claws. He imagined them being able to cross the line and torture humans day after day, year after year. He couldn't even take the dreams. If that were to become a reality... No way.

But then he thought of the joyful, peaceful feelings he had when talking to the Michael-being after his accident and the overwhelming love that had engulfed him. That was definitely something he wanted. Was it real, though? Or had it only been a figment of his imagination? Was that love a person? Was that love Jesus?

Christopher felt a presence to his left. It wasn't Terry. Terry was on his right. He looked, just to be sure. Yep. Terry was on his right. He was afraid to look to the left. With all the crazy things happening in his life right now, this could be anything. Probably something bad, with his luck. He was absolutely sure that he was the only one that could see it. He closed his eyes and wished it away. It stayed.

The presence felt familiar somehow. There was an emotional warmth radiating from it. Still, Christopher didn't look. Instead, he looked at Terry. Terry seemed unaware of anything or anyone else sitting on this curb, but Christopher asked him anyway.

"Terry, do you see...anyone else...or anything else...here...with us?"

Terry looked around. "No. Just us. Why?"

"No reason," said Christopher, still refusing to look to his right.

"Is it good? Or do you feel something evil?" Terry asked him.

"Good, I think," said Christopher. "But weird. Definitely weird."

"I think you might be feeling the presence of Jesus," Terry told him. "He's waiting for you."

"For me? Why me?" Christopher asked. "Who the heck am I? I'm no one special. In fact, I've done nothing to make Him love me or be proud of me. I've messed up my life pretty good."

"You are special to Him, though," said Terry. "Jesus loves every single one of us. He's waiting for you to choose Him. It sounds to me like He's been waiting for you for a while and you've been fighting it. Believe me, once you stop fighting, you'll wonder why you waited so long. Jesus is awesome. Your choice, though. No one will force you."

"I've seen…I've seen both sides," Christopher told him, remembering Johnny and Michael. "The one side was so much fun but turned sour and ugly when he thought I wasn't looking. The other never hovered, he was just present when I needed him and radiated light and love when it mattered."

"That sounds about right," said Terry. "Satan will do everything he can to prevent you from coming to Jesus. He will distract you in any way he can and lie to you, making you believe that this life is all there is so you might as well have fun and enjoy it. That's a lie, though. There is more—so much more. Once you turn away from that lie and toward Jesus, you will see."

"If, and I say IF, I wanted to believe and meet Jesus, how would I do that?" Christopher asked.

Terry told him.

"Are you ready to give your life to Jesus? Are you ready to meet Him?" Terry asked.

Christopher didn't answer right away.

"No. Not yet," he said finally. "I need to think about it." Yep, an alternate universe for sure. He just needed to get away from Terry, to get away from everyone and everything. He needed to wake up from this nightmare.

The presence on his right was still there, but fading. He stole a glance in that direction and saw a nebulous figure that looked a little like Michael disappear into nothingness. For some reason, he suddenly felt really, really sad.

CHAPTER 35

Johnny was having a party. Julian was there. Peter was there. Many other very handsome, very tall, very confident beings were there. There were shouts of congratulations and arguments about who should get credit for what going around the room.

"You did it. I doubted you could, but thanks to us, the mission succeeded!" crowed Julian. "The boss will be here soon to give us our rewards!" He was clearly excited.

"I told you, didn't I, that I would do it. Leave them alone and they'll come home," Johnny said in a sing-song voice.

"I thought outside the box, tailored it to the situation, and bada bing—done," he said proudly, gesturing toward himself with his hands.

A large dragon entered the room and everyone scattered to get out of the way of his spiky, swinging tail. They were suddenly not so boastful anymore, at least not out loud. The dragon brought a stench with him that permeated everything. His eyes were sharp and intelligent. Smoke curled out from his mouth as he spoke.

"Well done. Well done." The dragon's voice was rich and low. The tone belied the hate just underneath the surface of the words.

"To whom should the reward be given?" he asked.

Johnny stepped forward. "To me, O Great One," he said. "I accomplished the mission."

"And me." Julian pushed his way forward.

"And me," boomed Peter. "Johnny was not able to do any of it without my help."

"Ah, I see," said the dragon. "You are quite sure the boy has chosen…correctly?"

"Yes," said Johnny. "He has refused Je…. The false god's… invitation multiple times. He's done. He's ours, I mean yours. He's yours."

Christopher walked slowly back to his house. This past year had taken a toll on him. He was tired of the dreams. He was tired of the drugs. He was tired of school. He was tired of fighting. He was tired of everything. He wanted to just give up.

"He's mine when he's dead. Is he dead?" the dragon asked, looking accusingly around the room at all of the demons gathered there.

"Almost," replied Julian. "Almost."

Christopher had never felt so alone. He had pushed away his friends. He had pushed away his parents. He had pushed away everyone who tried to help him. He had no one left who cared. Heck, he didn't even care anymore. It seemed like everyone in his life was headed the opposite way than he was. "What's the use?" he thought aloud. "I'm done."

Christopher headed up the front steps. No one was home. Good. He went down into the basement and unlocked his father's gun safe. His dad had no idea he even knew the combination but he had memorized it long ago—just in case. Well, now was the "just in case."

He loaded one bullet in the chamber of a Smith&Wesson M&P 9 mm semiautomatic hand gun. He would just need one. Christopher sat down in a chair and put the barrel of the gun under his chin, pointed up.

Johnny giggled with glee. "Any second now. Any second!"

"Who is there to make sure? Who is there to bring him to me?" asked the dragon.

"I'll go!"

"No, me!"

"I'm better suited for that!"

"It's my job!"

"Me! Me! Me!"

The demons erupted in raucous arguments about who should go. While they did, Johnny slipped away.

"I've earned the right," he said to his boss.

"Yes," agreed the dragon. "Go."

Christopher laid the gun on his lap and began to cry. He wasn't sure where this was coming from. He never cried. But he was crying now. What he felt was beyond sad. Sad was how he felt when Nonno and Momma died. Sad was how he felt when Crystal wasn't around. This was not sad. This was total misery. This was absolute despair. He was being pulled in two directions so diametrically opposed that, if it were physical rather than mental, his arms would be ripped from their sockets.

What happens when your mind is being pulled apart? At this moment, Christopher felt there was only one way to stop it, to escape the anguish.

"I don't know what to believe," he sobbed. "If there is a God, you need to help me. Otherwise…" Christopher picked up the gun again. "Otherwise, I'm done. Nothingness is better than this. I can't take the mind games anymore. The nightmares. The aliens coming and going. Not knowing what is real or imaginary. All of it."

He felt the presence again. He felt a hand on his shoulder, but when he turned around to look, no one was there.

"See? Crazy. I am ab-so-lute-ly crazy. Certifiably insane."

Christopher put the gun back under his chin.

"Wait."

That sounded like Michael. In his head. A voice in his head. Great. Just great.

"Jesus is the way, Christopher. You know that. In your heart, you know that. You've seen the peace He's given to Crystal, to Tony, to your mom and dad. You can have that peace too."

Christopher just sat with the gun under his chin, listening for more. There was no more. It was eerily quiet both in his head and in the room. What was the truth? If there was nothing after death, then death would be better than what he was feeling now. But if there was a Heaven and a Hell...

He lowered the gun and bounced it up and down on his lap, keeping his finger near the trigger. He made his decision.

A shot rang out, echoing through the basement.

"No!" shouted Michael, appearing in the basement room in a flash of light.

"Yes!" shouted Johnny, coming in a split second later, sword drawn.

Johnny brought his sword forward, swinging it across the front of his body and stepping to the right to avoid the blow he knew was coming from Michael. Michael blocked the attack and countered with one of his own. His sword sliced through Johnny's sleeve and nicked the scaly skin underneath. Both angels attacked and parried without tiring. Neither could actually kill the other, but Michael's goal wasn't to kill anyway. It was to keep Johnny away from Christopher in these crucial moments.

Johnny wasn't thinking about a goal. He was mad with rage and hate and saw only the obstacle blocking his way. He forgot what that way was, temporarily.

When he remembered, Johnny stopped fighting and bolted toward Christopher. He no longer bothered to hide his true features. He stood before Christopher, enormous and hideous, reaching out his claws to claim him and return to the dragon.

Johnny stopped short, shocked and dismayed. Christopher was alive! How could this be? He had heard the shot. Christopher should be dead. Why wasn't he dead? Johnny was frantic. He couldn't fail. He mustn't fail.

The bullet was lodged in the wall across from where Christopher was sitting. Joseph had hung a variety of targets on either side of the gun cabinet, stored and ready to take with him to the gun range. One of those targets was a black shadow of an alien, facing forward with one leg extended as if he were about to step off the paper target and into the real world. Christopher had hit the adumbral paper alien in the chest, dead center.

Johnny paced back and forth, unsure what to do next. Michael stood next to Christopher, sword still drawn.

Christopher had his head turned upward and did not see either Johnny or Michael at all. He seemed calm now. He sighed in surrender and then spoke into the air.

"OK, Michael-in-my-head. I want that peace. I choose that peace over this turmoil for sure." Christopher said out loud. It felt good to say that. He meant it. He was smiling as he put the gun back in the gun safe and ran up the stairs.

Michael followed Christopher out the front door. Job done. Mission accomplished. The final name had just been added to the Book of Life. He spread his wings and spun upward through the clouds.

Johnny ran. He was scared of the dragon. He had failed. At the last second, he had failed. It wasn't his fault, he told himself. If those others had not spent precious seconds arguing about who should come, he would have been here in time. He had to hide. He had to go somewhere the dragon couldn't find him, and he would have to do it quickly. It would not take long for the dragon to find out. He spread his wings and flew west as fast as he could. Behind him, he heard a great roar, full of rage and hate.

On the front porch, at the top of the front steps, Christopher stretched out his arms as wide as he could and shouted, "I choose Jesus! Do you hear me? I choose Jesus!"

TJ pulled up to the curb in his truck, radio blaring. He knew Mr. and Mrs. D'Antoni were at work, so it was safe for him to stop by with more Oxy. It looked like Christopher was waiting for him on the porch. How did he know TJ would be coming by? Oh well, good luck and good timing, TJ supposed.

TJ rolled down the passenger window, turned down the radio, and called to Christopher, "Hey Chris, I've got…"

A loud noise like a thousand car horns blasting at the same time sounded all around him and drowned out his words. TJ put his hands over his ears and looked in his rearview mirror. There was nothing there! Nothing in front of him! What the heck had that been?

A flash of light lit up the sky. It was brighter than any lightning TJ had ever seen before. He looked out the window. Christopher was still there, hands raised, smiling and swearing. At least TJ thought it was swearing—Christopher was saying Jesus a lot.

TJ stared at him. What was wrong with that boy? Was he already high? He stared at his friend and tried to figure that out.

What the heck?! One second Christopher was there, the next second he was gone. Just gone. Disappeared. The front door hadn't opened, hadn't closed. TJ was quite sure he hadn't blinked. Even if he had, he could not have missed Christopher going in the house in just one blink.

The music on the radio stopped suddenly, replaced by static. Then, a news anchor came on the air and said reports were coming in that thousands of people all over the world had just disappeared. Vanished. No one was quite sure why yet, but the president was in conference with nine other world leaders and would give the public an update as soon as one was available. They were advising people to stay indoors and stay tuned.

TJ put his truck in gear and floored it, racing toward the highway. He had heard about this in Sunday School as a kid. He had heard about the rapture. He knew where Christopher had gone. He knew what was coming.

Epilogue

The dragon had only been this angry once before. He had mistakenly believed that killing Jesus would end the whole war and he could take his rightful place as King of the Universe. The only true God. King of this world wasn't good enough. He wanted it all. But to get it, he would have to eliminate God. He tried and failed to kill Him. Well, he had killed Him, but then he had had to fight Him in Sheol and lost. Jesus had defeated Death and rescued thousands of souls the dragon had trapped there, taking them all back to Heaven with Him.

The dragon had never even considered that possibility. No one had ever escaped death before so how could he have seen that coming? He had gone on a raging warpath for a millennium after that, destroying everything he could by spreading disease, inciting wars, causing earthquakes and floods, and anything else he could think of. After that, he calmed down enough to plan another strategy. The earth was his, after all. And he had an army of angels that had been kicked out of Heaven with him. They weren't the most loyal, but he could control them. There was no one more powerful than he was except, perhaps, God. We will see. We will see, he thought.

Humans were key. God loved them, so he hated them. God had made angels first—beautiful beings. He was the most beautiful, of course. The dragon knew that. They all knew that. Then God had to ruin a good thing by creating humans—in his own image. Little gods, looking just like daddy. But they sure didn't act like daddy! The dragon laughed. He had made sure of that. Humans were really stupid. Johnny had been right about that. Left to themselves, they messed things up all on their own with very little effort needed on his part.

Johnny! The dragon's rage returned. He would find Johnny and tear his head off. He couldn't hide forever. This earth was small.

Only one thing to do. One thing and he didn't do it. Keeping that last human from choosing Jesus was all it would take to keep this world going down the same path it had been going since Adam. But no, Johnny had failed to keep that boy from Jesus and look what happened! Now there were millions of humans and angels in Heaven preparing for the final battle. Well, they would not win.

The dragon knew he had seven years before they would come for him. He would be ready.

CPSIA information can be obtained
at www.ICGtesting.com
Printed in the USA
JSHW012330030523
41239JS00001B/3

9 781662 862410